# Grayson's gaze roved over my face in slow motion.

He studied my grey-green eyes for a heart-stopping moment. Then he shifted his focus to my mouth and paused there even longer. I was having trouble breathing. I had forgotten how to do it. My breath was locked somewhere in my throat as the seconds ticked on and on and on.

He strode purposely over to the door and opened it for me, standing to one side as I walked through. I was aware of the difference in our height as I walked past him. I was aware of the citrus and bergamot fragrance of his aftershave that was as intoxicating as a mind-altering drug. I was aware of his gaze following my every movement, making my body feel different somehow, more feminine, more graceful...desirable.

And I was acutely aware that I was the one who needed some solid sense talked into.

**Melanie Milburne** read her first Harlequin novel at the age of seventeen, in between studying for her final exams. After completing a master's degree in education, she decided to write a novel, and thus her career as a romance author was born. Melanie is an ambassador for the Australian Childhood Foundation and a keen dog lover and trainer. She enjoys long walks in the Tasmanian bush. In 2015 Melanie won the HOLT Medallion, a prestigious award honoring outstanding literary talent.

### Books by Melanie Milburne

### Harlequin Presents

*The Billion-Dollar Bride Hunt*

### *The Scandalous Campbell Sisters*

*Shy Innocent in the Spotlight*
*A Contract for His Runaway Bride*

### *Weddings Worth Billions*

*Cinderella's Invitation to Greece*
*Nine Months After That Night*
*Forbidden Until Their Snowbound Night*

Visit the Author Profile page
at Harlequin.com for more titles.

# Melanie Milburne

---

## ONE NIGHT IN MY RIVAL'S BED

Recycling programs
for this product may
not exist in your area.

ISBN-13: 978-1-335-73949-0

One Night in My Rival's Bed

Copyright © 2023 by Melanie Milburne

For questions and comments about the quality of this book,
please contact us at CustomerService@Harlequin.com.

Harlequin Enterprises ULC
22 Adelaide St. West, 41st Floor
Toronto, Ontario M5H 4E3, Canada
www.Harlequin.com

Printed in U.S.A.

# ONE NIGHT IN MY RIVAL'S BED

To Cliona Kennedy, who looks after our pets when we need her to. You are such a wonderful caretaker of our fur family and we appreciate you so much. We can truly relax with you in charge!

# CHAPTER ONE

I WAS MEETING my younger sister Niamh for a drink after work at one of London's swanky hotels. Now, you might think there is nothing unusual about two sisters catching up over a cocktail but it's nothing short of a miracle I still have a sister. It's also a miracle Niamh could not only book the venue but get there without her support worker. And it's an even bigger miracle I arrived at the hotel more or less on time.

I'm normally a super punctual person but my last client of the day wanted some changes to the plans I was drawing up for his luxury villa in Italy. Before you get too excited, the client is nudging eighty and he's building it for his grandchildren. Lucky grandchildren. The only thing I got from my paternal grandparents was a chip on my shoulder. Long story. I won't bore you with it.

I spotted Niamh sitting in the brass and glass mezzanine level area, surrounded by gorgeous fresh flower arrangements that made it look like summer had come inside. Which was kind of nice because even though it was June, summer certainly hadn't made much of an appearance outside. It had rained for twenty-two days in a row. But I live in hope.

I moved through the chairs and tables, and I noticed with a pulse-tripping jolt that Niamh was not alone. A stop-your-heart-handsome dark-haired man was beside her seated in a wheelchair. He looked vaguely familiar and I narrowed my gaze as I tried to place him. Neither he or Niamh were looking my way, they seemed completely absorbed in each other. Yikes! They were even holding hands.

Okay, so now you're probably wondering why I was so surprised to see my sister holding hands with a gorgeous-looking man. Why shouldn't my sister be happy in love or lust or whatever?

Because while my sister is twenty-seven years old, she is still in many ways a child and it is entirely my fault.

Niamh looked up and saw me standing there and waved me over with an excited gleam in her eyes. 'Ash, come and meet Ethan Barlowe. Ethan's older brother Grayson will be here soon.'

*Grayson Barlowe?* I had to force myself to walk without stumbling. I had to force myself to smile as if everything was okay. But everything was not okay. It was seriously not okay. Barlowe was not an uncommon name but…surely Ethan's brother couldn't be…? I swallowed a furry thickness in my throat and looked at Ethan's darkly handsome features again. That glossy black hair, those grey-blue eyes were so incredibly familiar, and yet Ethan had laughter lines I had never seen on Grayson Barlowe's face.

I offered my right hand to Ethan. 'Nice to meet you, Ethan.'

There was an awkward moment when he offered his left hand instead of his right but then I realised he couldn't use his right hand at all. It lay limply on his thigh. I noticed then that his wheelchair was a motorised one, no doubt because it would be impossible for him to wheel himself about without the use of both hands.

'Lovely to…m-m-meet you, Ash. Niamh's t-t-told me so much about…you.' Ethan's voice had a slight stutter and he paused and frowned fiercely in concentration before he said some words, as if his brain had trouble deciding which word to use. I'm an architect, not a neurologist, but I can recognise an acquired brain injury when I see it. Besides, for twenty years I've been managing my sister's.

There was the sound of someone approaching and I didn't need to turn around to see who it was. I could recognise that slightly uneven gait anywhere. A shiver ran down my spine like an ice-footed spider and my heart began to pound like I was having some sort of medical event. I caught a whiff of expensive aftershave, one I had smelled three months ago at the Architectural Awards event where I was pipped at the post by Grayson Barlowe, who took home the major award that I had coveted for months and stupidly thought would be mine. Not because of an overblown sense of my own creative ability but because so many of my colleagues had said my entry was sure to win. It didn't. And it particularly rankled that Grayson Barlowe had won it instead.

We've been business rivals for years. The rivalry didn't start with us, it started with his grandfather and my father. They were at war the entire length of their careers and even though they are both now deceased, the battle hadn't gone to the grave with them. Out of respect for my father, I continued to resent Grayson Barlowe and all he represented. Not that he isn't a creative genius. I've lost count of the number of awards he's won for his stunning and innovative designs. I'm just insanely jealous of his success that seems to come so easily to him. Oh, and the fact that he's a playboy who only has to look at a woman to get her to fall at his feet in a swoon. Not me, though. I'm fully vaccinated and completely immune against his polished brand of male charm.

'Grayson,' Ethan said, smiling broadly at his older brother. 'Come and meet my…my fiancée.'

'*Fiancée?*' Grayson Barlowe and I spoke in shocked unison—although his voice was low and deep and kind of raspy and sexy. Mine was more like the sound of someone inadvertently stepping on a squeaky toy.

Niamh's smile was even wider than Ethan's. She held up her left hand and an expensive-looking engagement ring flashed with brilliance that rivalled the sparkles in her eyes. 'Ethan proposed to me earlier this week. That's why we wanted you both here to celebrate with us this evening.'

I was having trouble finding my voice. I was having trouble believing my sister had met and fallen in love with someone without me knowing anything about it. I was having trouble standing next to Grayson Barlowe without dropping at his Italian leather clad feet in a swoon. He was wearing a charcoal-grey business suit that highlighted the width of his broad shoulders and the long lean length of his legs. His ink-black hair was swept back off his face similar to his brother's but, unlike Ethan, Grayson had flecks of grey at his temples, giving him a distinguished, older and wiser look that somehow made him even more attractive.

His ice-blue eyes met mine and a current of energy hit me like a lightning zap.

'Did you know anything about this?' There was

an accusatory quality to his voice that reminded me of a high school teacher I had a showdown with when I was fifteen. I wasn't so sure I could win a face-off with Grayson as my opponent, but I was going to have a red-hot go at it. But don't get me started about my combative nature.

'No, nothing. Did you?' I shot back.

Grayson's lips thinned into a grim flat line. 'Of course not.' He turned back to face his younger brother, a frown carved deeply between his eyes. 'How long have you known each other?'

'Six weeks,' Ethan said with a defiant light in his eyes.

'Six weeks!' Grayson and I did the speaking in unison thing again. Well, he spoke, I screeched like a startled cat.

I looked at Niamh. 'How can you be sure he's the one in such a short time?'

Niamh's chin came up and her eyes took on the same defiant gleam as Ethan's. 'We knew the minute we met each other at the gym. I thought you'd be happy for me. I haven't had a boyfriend before and Ethan is so kind and good and—'

'Rich.' The cynical note in Grayson's voice made me want to slap him. Not that I'm an advocate for violence of any sort but it riled me that he was suggesting my sister was a gold-digger. He had only just met her. How could he make such a snap assessment of her?

I swung around to face Grayson with a glare so hot I could have moonlighted as a welding machine. 'How dare you?'

Grayson's eyes glittered with the same cynicism I'd heard in his voice. A worldly cynicism that made me feel wrong-footed somehow, which was weird because if there was an award for being a hard-nosed cynic it would surely go to me.

'Come with me,' he said, jerking his head in the direction of the exit. 'I want to speak to you in private.'

There was no possibility of me saying no. I suspect there were very few women on the planet who could say no to Grayson Barlowe. Besides, I wanted to speak to him where Niamh and Ethan couldn't listen in. We had to stop this nonsense between our siblings before it went any further. In love with someone after only six weeks? It was ridiculous. Niamh was naïve and innocent and way too trusting. It had taken me three years to get engaged to Ryan, but of course it had ended in tears. His, not mine.

Grayson led me to a private room on the other side of the hotel. It was furnished as a sitting room—twin soft sofas in plush velvet, long elegant silk curtains at the windows with a pelmet above. There was an antique writing desk and chair set on one side of the room, bookshelves on the other. The carpet was ankle-deep and handwoven and it was a gorgeous shade of shell pink to match the silk curtains. It would have been a feminine room except for the cold marble statue of the hotel's founder placed near the window, as well as a stern-looking portrait hanging on one of the walls. Those beady eyes seemed to glare at us as we made our way in, as if to ask us why his peace was being disturbed. *Rest in peace, old man*, I said to myself. *This fight is none of your business*.

Grayson closed the door once we were inside with an ominous-sounding *clunk*. His eyes drilled into mine and I resisted the urge to look away. I balled my hands into tight fists, my spine ramrod-straight, my chin high—it had to be held high in order to maintain eye contact with him. He was well over six feet and I couldn't help recalling how my ex-fiancé hated it when I wore heels. I reckon I could wear stilts around Grayson Barlowe and still have to crane my neck.

'This has to stop and it has to stop now.' His voice had a determined edge to it, hinting at a personality not unlike my own. Once I make up my mind, that's it. I don't back down.

Although I agreed with him, I was unwilling to be on his side due to his insulting assumption my sister was a shallow gold-digger. I found myself looking for reasons for Niamh and Ethan to continue their relationship in spite of my own reservations.

'What's your main objection?' I injected my tone with cool crispness. 'They're both consenting adults.'

His dark eyebrows snapped together in a tight frown. 'My brother has obviously been blindsided by your sister's looks. And she clearly wants someone wealthy enough to take care of her.'

I know my sister is stop-the-traffic stunning, but it was insulting that Grayson couldn't see past Niamh's looks to her sweet, gentle and caring nature. 'Ahem, it's the twenty-first century. Women don't need a man to take care of them.' Call me a hypocrite but, feminist though I am, I sometimes fantasise about a man taking care of me. A man who would have my back and stand by me and encourage and support me. Who would love me for being me. Not a single man in my life past or present has ever done that for me, so you can see why it's just a fantasy on my part. *Sigh.*

Grayson's mouth tightened even further. 'I will not allow my brother to be exploited by someone who's only after a meal ticket.'

'She's not looking for any such thing.' I knew it wouldn't take him long to see how limited my sister was in some areas. Unlike his brother, Niamh has no visible disability but if you spend enough time with her it soon becomes apparent she has some limitations. Not physical but intellectual. She has a reading age of an eight-year-old. She can only do simple maths. She has a small working memory, so complicated tasks can easily overwhelm her. Her support worker has helped her enormously, and of course I do everything I can, especially since Mum died three and a half years ago. It's been Niamh and me against the world ever since and, let me tell you, it's not always a nice world for people with acquired brain injuries. Or their carers.

Grayson scraped his broad-spanned hand through the thickness of his hair. I stared in fascination at the deep grooves his fingers left behind. I started to think about those long, tanned fingers gliding down the bare skin of my arm, or my legs… I shivered, and then swallowed thickly and quickly realigned my shoulders and spine back into a stiff don't-mess-with-me pose. It's kind of become my default posture in life, to be honest. Always bracing myself for a fight. I had no idea why I was suddenly fantasising about Grayson Barlowe's fingers on my body. It'd been a long time since I'd been intimate with anyone but surely I could find someone a little more suitable than my number one business rival?

Grayson's eyes came back to mine and a frisson coursed through my body. He had arresting eyes, a glacial ice blue with tiny flecks of grey. They were fringed with thick and long eyelashes that gave me an instant pang of envy. I had to use three coats of mascara and an expensive lash serum to make my lashes even vaguely noticeable.

'What sort of work does your sister do?'

'She doesn't have full-time employment…as yet. She volunteers at a pet shelter.' I moistened my dry lips with the tip of my tongue and added, 'Is your brother employed?'

Grayson's eyes followed the movement of my tongue with an intense focus that made something soft and feathery flutter across the floor of my belly. He rapid blinked and screened his expression like a shutter being drawn on a window.

'He works for me in a part-time position.' His curt answer contained a weight of information about him. Information I suspect I was able to decode only because of my own situation with my sister. There was a world of regret, guilt, pain and quiet despair in Grayson's reply. A world I was all too familiar with and knew I could never leave, even though I wished I could turn back time and do everything differently at that playground twenty years ago.

Grayson suddenly frowned again. 'Are you okay?'

It was my turn to rapid blink as the sting of tears at the backs of my eyes took me by surprise. I was caught off-guard by his assessing look. I was caught off-guard by my spiralling emotions. Emotions I had stuffed so deeply inside myself I had almost forgotten they were there. Almost.

My baby sister wanted to get married and I couldn't allow her to do it. Or at least, not in such a hurry. Not until I could guarantee she knew what she was doing. She had no experience when it came to men. She had never had a boyfriend before. I had spent my life trying to protect her from further hurt after the one time I failed to protect her. I could not bear to see her in any sort of pain, and emotional pain is one of the worst to experience. I should know, I've experienced it for years.

I brushed one of my hands over my eyes in an impatient manner. 'I have hay fever. All those fresh flowers in the restaurant.'

He reached into his jacket pocket and took out a neatly folded snowy white handkerchief and held it out to me. I stared at it like it was something I had never seen before. But then, it had been years since I had seen one. Most people use tissues these days. Grayson's possession of a freshly laundered and neatly ironed handkerchief seemed to suggest he was a traditionalist at heart. Or maybe he was doing his thing for the environment, saving our forests from being made into paper.

'Take it.' His voice had that note of drill sergeant command in it again, which made me want to refuse on principle but I mentally did a stocktake of my tote bag hanging on my shoulder and

I wasn't sure I had any tissues in there. Tampons, breath mints, lip-gloss, paracetamol, hand sanitiser, swanky new business cards that had cost me a fortune... No tissues. Then I recalled I gave my last purse-sized pack to Niamh two days ago when she had a nose bleed and I had forgotten to replace them.

I took the handkerchief from him and my fingers accidentally brushed against his. A ripple of energy flowed from his body to mine like a live electric current. I held his handkerchief up to my eyes, dabbing at them and trying to decide if I should blow my nose to give more authenticity to my claim of experiencing hay fever. I decided against the nose blow. Unfortunately, I have never been a dainty nose-blower. Seriously, I could stand in for a fog horn.

Along with the cleanly laundered smell, his handkerchief held a trace of his aftershave fragrance—an alluring blend of bergamot and citrus, and male body heat. I lowered the handkerchief from my face and folded it into an even smaller square. I needed something to do with my hands because, right then, I was tempted to reach up and touch Grayson Barlowe's stubbly jaw. The dark regrowth generously peppered his chiselled jawline and my gaze was magnetically drawn to the sculpted perfection of his mouth. His lower lip had a sensual fullness, his top lip sharply defined as if his Maker had spent an inordinate amount of time getting it right, like a sculptor works on their career-defining masterpiece. It was a mouth that hinted at a passionate nature that was carefully, vigorously held in check but once unleashed could be dangerous.

I suppressed another shiver, trying not to think of how dangerous it would be to be in bed with Grayson Barlowe. Dangerous and exciting and mind-blowing.

I stuffed the handkerchief in my tote bag. 'I'll wash it and get it back to you.'

'Keep it.'

I shrugged as if I didn't care either way, but I have a thing about returning borrowed things to their owners. Good manners and all that. Speaking of manners… Grayson and I had been invited to share in the celebration of Niamh and Ethan's engagement, but here we were behind a closed door instead of raising our glasses to their happy union in the flower-filled restaurant.

'So, what do you plan to do about your brother's engagement?'

'Stop it, that's what.'

I raised one of my eyebrows in an imperious arc. 'And how do you plan to do that?'

He let out a harsh-sounding breath that made his nostrils flare. He reminded me of a thoroughbred stallion ready to fight for his territory. 'I'll talk some sense into him.'

I gave a cynical twist of a smile. 'Good luck with that. He looks quite smitten with my sister.'

Grayson's expression hardened like quick-setting concrete. 'You can't seriously believe they're in love with each other?'

'Maybe they're in lust.' I immediately wished I hadn't mentioned *that* particular L word. I could feel my cheeks blooming with heat, as if by the very mention of the erotic word I had allowed something forbidden into the room. Something forbidden and dangerously tempting. Something that threatened to get out of control like a lit match to dry tinder. I could almost hear it crackling in the silence like tiny flames gathering energy to start an inferno.

His eyes held mine in a lock that sent a hot shiver rolling down my spine like a burning ember. I don't think I've ever had a man look at me quite so intensely. The air seemed charged with tension, a throbbing tension that increased as each heart-stopping second passed. He broke the eye contact and his gaze dipped to my mouth. And stayed there for endless seconds…

I held my breath.

My pulse quickened and my blood pumped and my heart jumped.

Grayson licked his lips and swallowed, returning his now inscrutable gaze to mine. 'Whatever they're feeling, I know it won't last.'

'You don't believe in true love?'

'Do you?'

I know I do it myself at times, but I hate it when people answer a question with a question. I suspected Grayson was very good at deflection. He wasn't the sort of man to give too much away about his feelings or his personal life. I gave a stiff smile that didn't show the brilliant job my cosmetic dentist had done on my once crooked teeth. It's taken me years to learn to smile properly but I still only keep them for special occasions.

'Some people get lucky.'

He glanced at my bare ring finger. 'You didn't?'

That's another thing I hate—how so many people in the architectural community knew about my broken engagement. But I guess, since I broke it off only days before the wedding it did kind of cause a bit of a scandal.

'Let's say I had a lucky escape.'

Grayson made a soft snorting noise but I couldn't tell if it was one of amusement or cynicism or something else. He was standing at least a metre away but I could still feel the male energy coming off him. A potent energy that made me aware of my femininity in ways I had never been to that degree before. My skin prickled, my heart raced, and liquid heat pooled in my dark secret places. Places I didn't want to think about right now. Places I hadn't thought about in years. I hadn't had a lover since my ex. I hadn't even felt a flicker of desire…until now. But what was I thinking? Sleeping with the enemy was a no-no. Besides, I couldn't afford to get distracted away from the issue of my sister and her…*gulp*…fiancé.

Grayson placed his hands on the back of the sofa he was standing behind and set his glittering gaze back on mine. 'Are we on the same page about getting Ethan and your sister to rethink their relationship?'

'How do you suggest we do that?' I knew my response hadn't actually answered his question but I was unwilling to commit to anything that would hurt my sister. Niamh believed herself to be madly in love. She was thrilled with the giant bauble on her ring finger. She had been dreaming about getting swept off her feet since she was a kid. The fact she was still a kid in some ways didn't mean she wouldn't be shattered if Grayson and I forced her to give up her dream of living happily ever after with Ethan.

Who was I to burst her big fragile shiny bubble and break up what could be her first and only chance to have a relationship? It was my fault she was the way she was and, while I was committed to protecting her and providing for her, I didn't want to sabotage her happiness. She deserved to be loved. Didn't everyone? And while I wasn't entirely sure of Ethan's motives, on the surface he looked like he was absolutely besotted by her. But that might be a temporary infatuation. It might fade and then my sister's heart would be broken and I would have to pick up the pieces.

Not that I'm without considerable experience in that department—my mother fell apart when my father took his life after a business deal went wrong a couple of years before Niamh's accident. A business deal with Grayson Barlowe's grandfather, no less. Hence the ongoing feud between the Clancy and Barlowe camps. My father's death was as unexpected as the failed business deal that left us basically penniless. Mum fell apart, even though she and my father had had a rocky relationship at the best of times. I finally managed to get her back on her feet but then she fell to pieces again when Niamh was injured, which was totally understandable. It was a double blow to lose her husband and then have her favourite child permanently damaged in the space of two years. To say I'd had to grow up fast is an understatement. There wasn't time to process my own grief. I was too busy carrying my guilt.

'We sit down with them and talk them through the issues.' Grayson's voice cut through my painful thoughts.

*We?* He wanted me to join forces with him? The

thought of teaming up with him gave me a weird feeling in my stomach. A kind of shivery feeling that was part thrill, part dread. I sat on the sofa, not because I wanted to but because my legs were feeling a little unsteady. Grayson's presence was so intimidating and yet I couldn't take my eyes off him. He was so damn attractive, even when he was frowning.

'Issues such as?'

His eyes hardened to flint. 'My brother has a trust fund left to him by our late grandfather.'

I upped my chin a fraction. 'So?'

'I don't want him to be taken advantage of by a supposedly love-struck beautiful young woman. It wouldn't be the first time it's happened.'

Anger was a fire in my blood that threatened to boil its way out of my veins. 'My sister is not the type of person to be influenced or impressed by how much money a man has. She's not the least bit mercenary or worldly.' I wanted to say *And nor am I*, but it didn't seem relevant at that moment. I wasn't interested in impressing him with my self-sufficiency. I just wanted to protect my sister from being hurt by his ruthless approach to the situation.

'It's obvious Ethan's been taken in by her act of doe-eyed innocence,' Grayson said, moving away from the sofa. He opened and closed his hands, as if trying to release some tension. 'He's not mentioned a word to me about dating anyone and now suddenly he's freaking engaged? She must have made him promise to keep it a secret.'

I widened my eyes in outrage, even though, like him, I was a little peeved Niamh hadn't told me a thing about dating Ethan either. I was used to knowing *everything* about her, far more than most older sisters would know. But then I've had to know everything in order to make sure she has all she needs and to keep her from being exploited by others.

'Look, I don't know the full extent of your brother's disability but I think you're doing both he and Niamh a disservice without a proper conversation with them first.'

'Marriage is out of the question. I'll do everything in my power to stop it.' His adamant tone riled me more than it should have. It was like I was programmed to adopt the opposite stance even though I actually agreed with him. But then he was a Barlowe, and I was a Clancy. We had a long history of going head to head.

I rose from the sofa and nailed him with my gaze, still playing devil's advocate. 'You know, some people do actually fall in love quite quickly. Or don't you believe in love at first sight?'

His mouth slanted in a smile right out of the cynical playboy's playbook. 'No. But lust at first sight? Yes.'

There was a pulsing silence. A silence so intense that I could just about hear my own heart beating. I could certainly feel it hammering away in my chest like an industrial piston.

Grayson's eyes roved over my face in slow motion. He studied my grey-green eyes for a heart-stopping moment. Then he shifted his focus to my mouth and paused there even longer. I was having trouble breathing. I had forgotten how to do it. My breath was locked somewhere in my throat as the seconds ticked on and on and on. Niamh is always saying what a nice mouth I have. I am less complimentary about my features. But right then, with Grayson Barlowe's gaze staring at my mouth as if it were the most beautiful and fascinating mouth in the world, I was starting to wonder if I needed to reassess my opinion on my physical assets.

But suddenly, as if someone had snapped their fingers to break a spell, Grayson shifted his gaze and glanced at the door. 'We'd better get back to the restaurant and talk some sense into them.'

He strode purposefully over to the door and opened it for me, standing to one side as I walked through. I was aware of the difference in our height as I walked past him. I was aware of the citrus and bergamot fragrance of his aftershave that was as intoxicating as a mind-altering drug. I was aware of him following my every movement, making my body feel different somehow, more feminine, more graceful...*desirable*.

And I was acutely aware that *I* was the one who needed some solid sense talked into them.

# CHAPTER TWO

WE MADE OUR way back to the restaurant but when I looked at the table where Niamh and Ethan had been sitting it was now occupied by another group of people. I swivelled my gaze around the restaurant but there was no sign of my sister and her... Ethan. I still couldn't bring myself to refer to him as her fiancé. Niamh was mentally too young to be married. Too naïve to know what she was doing. I had to stop her from screwing up her life and I had to do it now.

I swung around to look up at Grayson. 'Where are they?' My voice was kind of scratchy as panic climbed up my spine.

His frown carved a deep trench between his eyes and he muttered a filthy curse not quite under his breath. 'They can't have gone far. Wait here. I'll ask the staff.'

I'm not used to being ordered around but this time I did as I was told. The thunderous expression on Grayson's face was enough to freeze me on the spot. For a decade.

But while he was off interrogating the staff, I did my own investigation. I pulled out my phone from my tote bag and opened the app that could locate my sister's whereabouts within seconds. But for some reason Niamh was not showing up any more. She had either turned off her phone or blocked me from keeping track of her. I didn't even realise she knew how to do that. Or had Ethan done it for her? My sister could be impulsive at times, it was one of the things that had changed about her personality since the accident. One of many things that had changed. But, until now, I had always managed to stop her from doing anything rash.

How could I stop her if I didn't even know where she was?

Grayson came back to me with an even more furious expression. 'They left the restaurant soon after we left them to talk privately. Damn it. I should've known something like this would happen.'

My heart was thumping like I'd been administered with a shot of adrenalin. It threatened to beat its way out of my ribcage. 'We didn't leave them for long. Is Ethan able to drive? Or did they come in a cab or rideshare?'

A flicker of something passed over Grayson's face, something I recognised because I had seen it on my own face for the last twenty years just about every time I looked in a mirror. A flash of pain, a ripple of regret, a gnawing ache of guilt. The trifecta of ghastly feelings one has when one feels totally responsible for a loved one's injuries. I had heard about the serious car crash Grayson and Ethan were involved in when Ethan was a teenager. Someone had mentioned it to me at an architectural conference but they hadn't given me many details and I was too polite to dig for more information. Besides, I didn't want anyone to think I was showing too much interest in my business rival's background. But, as far as I knew, Ethan had been the one driving. Or did Grayson blame himself for not insisting on driving himself?

'No, he no longer drives. What about your sister?'

'No. She mostly uses public transport or I take her where she needs to go. Oh, and sometimes her support worker.'

Grayson looked at me oddly for a moment. 'She has a support worker?'

'Yes, not a full-time one, though. She only needs help with some tasks, I fill in the rest.'

A perplexed frown wrinkled his brow. 'I didn't realise she was disabled.'

'Most people don't until they spend some time with her. She has an acquired brain injury from an accident when she was seven.' I didn't tell him the rest of the story. The horror story that had changed my family for ever. I had turned my back for only thirty seconds while she was on the swing, possibly even less time than that, and yet it had been enough for her to fall off and fracture her skull. Those few seconds had changed everything for all of us, most of all for Niamh. Her potential stolen. Her brain no longer functioning the way it was meant to.

Grayson sent his hand through the thickness of his hair again and I wondered if it was a stress thing. A habit he had adopted without realising it.

'I'm sorry.' His voice was deep and rusty. 'I thought she was yet another gold-digger after Ethan's trust fund.'

'But she told you she met Ethan at the gym. It's a specialised one that has tailor-made classes for each client.'

His jaw worked for a moment as if he was mentally chewing over something. 'I thought she might be a care worker or fitness trainer or something. Ethan was taken in by a carer a couple of years ago. He was convinced she was the real deal but, of course, she wasn't. She knew about his trust fund and wanted to set herself up in life. I knew what would happen. A costly divorce in a year or two's time. I paid her off in the end. It was cheaper and easier and saved a fortune on legal fees.'

'How did Ethan take it?'

'He was shattered.'

'I'm sorry to hear that, but I can assure you Niamh will not break your brother's heart.'

Grayson's eyes glinted with his trademark cynicism. 'Not if I can help it, she won't.'

I tightened my mouth and glared back at him. 'Firstly, you won't be able to pay her off.'

One dark brow rose in a perfect arc. 'How about you?'

I stared at him for a thumping heartbeat or two. What was he implying? That I could be paid to go away and take my sister with me?

'You think you can write a cheque to get rid of me? Think again.'

He moved closer and looked down from his considerable height into my upturned face. I stood, totally mesmerised. I wanted to look away but I couldn't. My body was disconnected from my brain. My brain was saying, *Step back, put some distance between him and you*, but none of it was getting through. The Wi-Fi was down or something, or too weak to pick up the message. And I was too weak to do anything but look into his darkly handsome features. I was transfixed by the intractable light in his eyes, by the sudden flare of his nostrils, by the alluring smell and heat of him that dazzled my senses as no one had ever done before.

'How do I know you're not behind them getting

together?' he said, through thinned lips. 'For all I know, you've probably facilitated their getaway, all the while pretending to be as surprised by their announcement as me.'

I was shocked by his cynical assessment of me, shocked and angry, but I was keen to keep a lid on my emotions. He was a powerful opponent and I didn't want to give him any advantage by behaving like I had zero emotional regulation. But right then I wanted to swing a savage kick at his shins. I wanted to scrape my nails down his too-handsome face. I wanted to grab a fistful of his hair and tug and tug and tug. Another secret part of me wanted to grab the front of his crisp business shirt and lift my mouth to meet his hard one.

But, instead, I drew in a quiet and calming breath and held his gaze with cool composure. 'I'm as completely in the dark as you. And we're losing valuable time arguing the point here.'

He held my gaze for a long pulse-stopping moment. Then he let out a harsh-sounding breath and raised one of his hands to the knot of his tie, tugging at it as if it was choking him. 'I need to find my brother before he does something he later regrets.'

'At least we live in London, not Las Vegas. If so, they could have been married by an Elvis impersonator by now.'

Grayson didn't appear to appreciate my attempt

at humour. He glared at me so darkly I thought I might turn on the spot to smouldering ashes. Or maybe it was because I was already feeling so hot in his disturbing presence. I'm no naïve innocent like my sister but I have never met someone who stirs my senses into such a frenzy. I'm normally so logical and sensible but I had trouble keeping my thoughts in order. My brain kept coming up with X-rated images of Grayson Barlowe and me in bed together, naked limbs entangled, his muscled arms and legs pinning me to the mattress. Or the floor, or the ground, or up against a wall…

I gave a tiny shudder and gave myself a con-cussion-inducing mental slap. I had to stop think-ing about him in such an erotic way. He wasn't my type and I was certainly not his. I'd seen him in the gossip pages, and at awards events, with blonde bombshells who looked so perfectly put together they could have been supermodels. Some of them *were* supermodels. Interestingly, Niamh is a blonde bombshell with her white-blonde hair and stunning figure. I haven't cracked any mirrors lately but I can safely say I do not look anything like a supermodel. Not even close. I fall into the category of mousy girl next door. Or maybe girl down the road, so far down the road you wouldn't notice her at all.

Grayson shoved his shirt cuff back to check his designer watch. My gaze was drawn to the dark hairs that covered his wrists and tapered over the backs of his hands and long strong fingers. He glanced back at me and my heart skipped and tripped.

'We'd better check Ethan's apartment first, then we can widen the search.'

'We?'

'Yes, we. It will be quicker if we stick together. Besides, I don't want you out of my sight until I'm sure of your motives.'

I gave him a gelid look. 'I can assure you my motives are the same as yours. Exactly the same.'

Grayson's brows rose ever so slightly and a devilish glinting light appeared in his gaze that made my pulse pick up its pace like a runner dashing for the finish line.

'So you want the same as me.' It was a statement not a question, but I wasn't so sure he was still talking about his brother and my sister. The electric energy was back in the air again, fizzing around us like a wayward current. Tingles ran up and down my spine, hot little pinprick tingles that made me aware of my escalating pulse and increased breathing rate. Seriously, I had to either get fit or get laid. Eek, why was I always thinking about sex around this man?

'I want to find my sister before your brother breaks her heart,' I said. 'I'm sure he's a nice guy and all that but she has no experience around men.'

Grayson moved towards the exit, signalling for me to follow him. 'Come on then. We'll try Ethan's place first and go from there.'

A few minutes later, I drew up behind Grayson's car outside a block of apartments in a lovely tree-lined street in Islington. Before I could unclip my seatbelt he was by my driver's door, opening it for me. I didn't know whether to be flattered or furious. The feminist in me insisted I was perfectly capable of opening my own door, thank you very much. But another part of me lapped up the old-world chivalry with relish.

Grayson led the way to the entrance of the building. He typed some numbers into a keypad and the doors opened. We walked across the shiny marble foyer to the lift and he pressed the call button and the doors whispered open at his command.

He waved me to go ahead of him. 'After you.'

I stepped into the lift and he followed and the doors locked us in together. I was doing my best to avoid his gaze but my eyes kept tracking back to his face as if drawn by a magnetic force. He was still frowning, the twin pleat between his brows deep and tight enough to grip a pencil.

'Does your brother live alone?'

'Yes, he insisted on it a couple of years ago. He has a support worker to help him in the morning to get ready for work but he spends the rest of his time alone.' His jaw tightened like a clamp and he added, 'Or so I thought.'

The lift stopped on the top floor and the doors opened on another gentle whisper. Grayson held the lift door open with one muscular arm while I stepped past him, conscious of his inscrutable gaze on me, and doing my level best not to trip or fall flat on my face.

He led the way to an apartment down the wide carpeted corridor and then pressed some more numbers into another keypad outside the door.

'Wait. Aren't you going to knock or ring the doorbell first?' I asked. 'Ethan and Niamh might be…you know…busy.' As euphemisms go, busy didn't quite cut it but I was determined not to mention the word 'sex' in front of him. I could already feel the heat in my cheeks and in my lower body.

Grayson glanced down at me, still frowning. 'Right…' He pressed the doorbell with his eyes still holding mine. Then, when there was no answer, he arched one dark eyebrow. 'Do I have your permission to enter now?'

I wasn't one hundred percent sure if he intended it as a double entendre but, all the same, I could feel myself flushing to the roots of my hair.

'Yes,' I said and blushed all the more because I was starting to think if he asked me to have sex with him I might indeed say yes. Not because I was interested in a relationship with him—I was over long-term relationships with men. But I figured it would be kind of interesting to experience a one-night stand with Grayson Barlowe. For research purposes. To see if the chemistry I was sensing between us was a real thing or a figment of my imagination.

The apartment door opened. The penthouse apartment door, actually. I tried not to look too impressed at the stunning décor, or gape at the view of Finsbury Park out of the large bank of windows in the spacious sitting room. I see gorgeous houses and apartments all the time. Many of them I've designed myself. I earn a very comfortable living and I've paid heaps off my pretty little townhouse's mortgage but it could be years and years before Niamh and I could ever live in a penthouse. Or have a view over a park.

Well, it seems Niamh could do if she married Ethan Barlowe. *Just saying...*

I pushed the thought away as quickly as it formed. My sister could *not* rush into marriage after only six weeks. She didn't know Ethan well enough. Marrying someone was a big commitment, and there were issues to consider regarding their levels of disability. Issues they might not have thought through in the heady rush of falling madly in love. If indeed they had fallen in love. I've had my fair share of infatuations over the years, so I understood how convincing those feelings can be at the time.

Grayson wandered through the apartment but I stayed put in front of the windows overlooking the park. I chewed my lower lip, mentally working through some of the issues the young couple might have to face. They both had disabilities that might impact on how they lived together. Surely they needed to spend a little more time considering how well-suited they were *before* they got married? It's too late once the ink is dry on a marriage certificate. I wish my parents had thought a little more about it before they said, 'I do.' Of course, in blindingly bright hindsight, I now realise I too should have considered whether or not Ryan and I were as well-suited as I wanted us to be. But I was in stubborn denial and had my head buried so deep in the sand I'd hit water and I couldn't see through the bubbles for how bad things actually were.

'They're not here.' Grayson spoke from behind me.

I turned to face him, struck again by how flipping gorgeous he looked even when he was frowning and glaring.

'Where else could they have gone?'

'Your sister's place?'

'Niamh lives with me.'

His hands were resting on his slim hips and his frown deepened. 'And you *still* didn't know anything about Ethan and her being involved?' The heavy scepticism in his tone annoyed me.

My back straightened, my gaze blazed, my blood boiled. 'Why do you keep suggesting I've colluded with them over their relationship? I had absolutely no idea she was seeing him. How do you know it wasn't him manipulating her, hmm?' I folded my arms in a defensive pose and added, 'That's the more likely scenario, in my opinion.'

'So when and where have they been alone together?' He seemed to be saying it to himself rather than me, his right hand going to his head to do that finger-combing thing again.

'Maybe they haven't been alone together a lot. Maybe you don't need to be when you meet The One.'

Grayson's steely gaze came back to mine and my stomach shivered like a shaken jelly. 'Since you have more experience than I do in such matters, I'll have to take your word for it.'

'Actually, my ex wasn't The One,' I found myself confessing. I unfolded my arms and dropped them by my sides and sighed. 'I just pretended to myself for way too long that he was.' Even three years on, I still cringe at how stupid I was to think Ryan and I were going to be together for ever.

'Who broke it off?'

'I did.'

There was a beat or two of silence.

'Why?' Grayson asked.

'He didn't want Niamh to be my bridesmaid.'

His eyebrows rose ever so slightly. 'Good call. You were together for what, a year or two or more?'

I was secretly impressed he didn't question the curtain coming down on my relationship but I wondered how he knew how long I had been going out with my ex. Ryan worked in the financial sector. He had no interest in architecture—another madly flapping red flag I should have noted earlier. I hadn't taken Ryan to any architectural awards ceremonies after the first time I was nominated for an award early in our relationship. He'd drunk too much because he was nervous for me—or so he said. Looking back now, I think he'd drunk because he was jealous of the attention I received.

'Three, actually. But it wasn't just about that.'

'What was it about?' Grayson's voice had softened to a gentle burr of sound that did strange things to my heart rate. As far as I know, I haven't got a heart condition but when I'm around Grayson Barlowe I swear I could have a hole in my heart or a murmur or a leaky valve, or all three.

'Ryan didn't understand my commitment to my sister. That she was always going to be a part of my life, especially after our mother died. Niamh needs me to watch out for her, to protect her from being exploited. We're a package deal. Buy one, get one for free.'

He lifted a dark eyebrow. 'Buy?'

'Bad choice of word but you know what I mean.'

Grayson let out a long sigh. 'Yes, I do indeed.'

There was another immeasurable silence. A silence in which I was conscious of only one thing—Grayson's blue eyes holding mine.

I licked my suddenly dry lips and he tracked the movement of my tongue with his hooded gaze. Something fizzed and tingled at the backs of my knees like a cocktail of sherbet and champagne had been injected into my bloodstream. I could feel it working its way through my body, sending tingling sensations to my core. Not the core I concentrate on during Pilates but that *other* core. The feminine core that most of the time I ignore.

But then the spell was broken when Grayson's phone began to ring. He grimaced and slid his hand into his jacket pocket, glancing at the screen before saying to me, 'Excuse me.' He turned slightly away to answer it. 'Mum?'

Okay, I admit it, I'm a terrible eavesdropper. Good manners aside, I just can't help myself. I do it all the time. Coffee shops, restaurants, the supermarket, museums, the gym, even walking along the street, I listen in on other people's conversations. I find them fascinating and revealing, sometimes even inspiring. Of course, I've perfected the art of eavesdropping, like now, for instance. I moved a short distance away—my hearing is good but not superhuman—and picked up a book that was on the coffee table, pretending an avid interest in robots.

'You *knew* about this?' Grayson's voice was loud enough to hear from outer space. Only joking. He didn't seem the type to shout at anyone, much less his mother. But his tone was certainly stern and disapproving. 'How can you encourage them? They've only known each other six weeks.'

It seems I underestimated the superhuman powers of my hearing because I could clearly hear Grayson's mother's response. 'How could you deny Ethan this chance to have a life with someone? He's in love and he wants to get married.'

'Have you met her? Niamh?' Grayson barked back, frowning like he was auditioning for a role as Chief Frowner.

'Yes, I have, as a matter of fact. I met them for lunch a few days ago. Niamh was charming and sweet and is obviously very much in love, and so is Ethan,' his mother said. 'Don't ruin it for him, Grayson. He deserves to be happy. He's been miserable for so long but now he's got his old spark back, and it warms my heart to see it.'

I saw a flicker of emotions pass over Grayson's face. His jaw worked, his eyes flinched as if the light was suddenly too bright and his broad shoulders tensed, as if the invisible weight he was carrying was finally wearing him down. He lifted a hand to his face and pinched the bridge of his nose, his shoulders now hunched forward.

'Look, I understand you want him to be happy. So do I. But he's rushing into this without doing due diligence. I think he should slow down a bit. Spend a bit of time getting to know Niamh and her circumstances a little better.'

'Niamh is nothing like Donna,' his mother said.

'And you've made that assessment after only one lunch meeting?' Grayson shot back.

'I'm a good judge of character.'

He gave a cynical sound that wasn't quite a laugh. 'Your track record on choosing husbands isn't great.'

There was a tight silence.

'I loved your father and he loved me. The accident changed everything. Your father couldn't cope with seeing both of you so badly injured.'

'I only broke my leg.'

'Everything that was you before that night was broken in that accident, Grayson.' His mother's voice had softened but I could still hear it. 'And of course, Ethan changed irreparably too. Your father couldn't handle it. He still can't. It's why he limits his contact with both of you.'

'How can you excuse his behaviour after all this time?' Grayson's voice was so bitter I could almost taste it in the air. 'He cheated on you, repeatedly, while Ethan's life was hanging in the balance.'

'Because somewhere underneath all that pain and anguish is the man I fell in love with.'

'Yes, well, that man is now shacked up with a new wife and family,' Grayson said through lips pulled so tight I could see the white tips at the corners of his mouth. 'His *perfect* family.'

See what I mean about eavesdropping? You find out so much information about people. I was intrigued by Grayson's backstory, not just about the accident and how it impacted his family but the comment about his father's new family. The way Grayson leaned on the word 'perfect' in such a scathing way. I know from experience that a lot of people find a disability in someone else confronting. Even small children stop and stare and ask questions that are hard at times to answer. Of course, adults should love their children no matter what. Had Grayson's father found the changes to his son Ethan all too difficult and sought comfort elsewhere?

It is a challenging time when the full extent of a patient's disability is made clear by the medical professionals. It can be devastating to find out your child can no longer do the things you dreamed and hoped they would do. Even as a sibling I found it nothing short of heartbreaking to see how Niamh's injuries permanently changed her, especially when it was my negligence that had caused them.

It sounded like Grayson's mother had a far more forgiving and accommodating nature than Grayson. How could she still have feelings for the man who had deserted her and her sons at their most vulnerable? To be perfectly honest, I lean a bit more towards Grayson's camp of unforgiving hard-nosed cynicism.

Forgiveness is definitely not my second name. It's Florence.

# CHAPTER THREE

GRAYSON WAS STILL frowning as he asked his mother, 'Do you have any idea where Ethan and Niamh are now? We left them for a few minutes at the restaurant, where they'd asked us to meet them, but when we got back they'd disappeared.'

'*We?*' his mother asked, like she was a detective homing in on a suspect's conflicting evidence.

Grayson glanced at me and then rolled his eyes. 'Niamh's older sister Ashleigh.'

'Ash,' I interjected quickly. No one ever calls me by my full name. Only my father called me Ashleigh and since he's been gone I can't bear hearing it on anyone else's lips.

'Is she against their relationship too?' his mother asked in an affronted tone.

'We both have some serious concerns, yes,' Grayson said.

'Well, I'm not sure I should tell you in case you try and ruin things for them,' his mother said.

'We don't want to ruin anything,' Grayson said with a note of frustration in his voice. 'We just want them to slow down a bit.'

'So says the man who changes lovers by the week, or even less,' his mother said with a generous dollop of disapproval.

'We're not talking about me, we're talking about Ethan,' Grayson said, pinching the bridge of his nose again until his tanned skin turned white under the pressure.

'Ethan is an adult. He might have a disability but he can decide how to live his life and if he wants to spend it with Niamh, who are you and her sister to oppose it? I don't want to see him end up alone and lonely…or give up…' The quality of his mother's voice changed over those three little revealing words, 'or give up.' Had Ethan tried to end his life after his last relationship ended? Grayson had said his brother was shattered by the previous breakup. That was understandable, given he had been set up and exploited by his carer. But shattered to what extent? To the point of wanting to end it all?

Niamh had dipped in and out of depression a couple of times over the years, wondering if anyone would ever love her the way she was. I had always supported her through those dips in mood and was always watching out for another one. Believe me, after losing our father to suicide, I have become extremely hypervigilant about subtle shifts in mood. But over the last six weeks I'd become a little more relaxed about her. She had been happier and more positive in her outlook than I had seen her in years. I'd put it down to the very expensive psychologist I had organised for her. But clearly it had more to do with Ethan Barlowe. Maybe I needed to be a little more positive about their relationship. It wasn't just money and security Ethan could give my sister—he could provide emotional support. Love. Commitment.

Grayson ended the call with his mother a short time later. He slipped the phone back in his jacket pocket and looked at me in a world-weary fashion. 'I'm sorry you had to listen to that.'

'I wasn't listening,' I said. I'm actually quite a good liar. I can control all the so-called tells people watch out for—the micro expressions that give most people away. But I got the feeling I wasn't fooling Grayson Barlowe. He held my gaze for a long moment, the silence stretching, stretching, stretching…

Then he looked at my mouth and I had the sudden urge to moisten my lips. I rolled my lips together instead and he continued to stare at my mouth as if it was something of unique and profound interest to him.

His gaze came back to mine and my heart

skipped a beat at the bright gleam in his eyes. 'What if they didn't go far when we left them?'

I was having trouble keeping up. I was so focused on that gleam in his eyes and wondering if he was going to kiss me.

'Erm…' I chewed at my lower lip, not sure of what to say, which, let me tell you, is way out of character for me. I am never lost for words.

'What if they stayed where they were?'

I frowned in confusion. 'But they weren't in the restaurant. I looked at every table. Besides, the wait staff told us they'd left the restaurant.'

'Not in the restaurant but in the hotel?'

Now I understood the gleam in his eyes—he thought he had solved a mystery. I was a little annoyed I hadn't thought of the possibility of Ethan and Niamh booking a room myself. It made sense they couldn't have gone far with Ethan's mobility issues.

'But how will we find out for sure? The hotel reception staff won't release private information about their guests,' I pointed out.

'I'm Ethan's legal guardian. They will have to tell me.'

'How come you're his guardian and not your mother or father?'

'My father wasn't interested, and my mother didn't want to do it on her own, so she signed it over to me.'

'Why?'

'Because I insisted.'

I raised my eyebrows. 'And no one ever says no to you?'

His eyes locked on mine with a searing heat that sent liquid fire through my blood. 'Occasionally.'

The atmosphere tightened. My heart rate escalated. My skin prickled and my palms moistened. Grayson's gaze dipped to my mouth and this time I didn't resist the urge to sweep the tip of my tongue across my lips. I couldn't resist. It was beyond my self-control. He triggered in me a desire so ferocious and feral it frightened me as much as it excited me.

But I had to stay in control. I couldn't allow myself to be distracted by a man like Grayson Barlowe.

'You know, I really thought you were going to do something really stupid back then,' I said in a voice far huskier than I'd intended.

Grayson quirked an eyebrow. 'Like what?'

I turned to pick up my tote bag from where I had left it on the floor near the sofa. I hung the strap of my bag over my left shoulder and glanced at him again but his expression was masked. Could I have misread the situation? Was I imagining the spark of chemistry that fired between us? I raised my chin a fraction, my gaze steady on his. 'I thought you were going to kiss me.'

A half-smile began to play about the corners of his mouth. It made him look even more devastatingly attractive and irresistible, especially as it set off a diamond-bright glint in his blue eyes. 'Do you really think I'd complicate things by doing something like that?'

I gave a one-shoulder shrug. 'I don't know you well enough to answer that question.'

Suddenly he wasn't standing two metres away but was right in front of me. I had to crane my neck to maintain eye contact. I had to control my ridiculous urge to wrap my arms around him and bring him even closer. I had to stop myself from staring at his mouth but looking into his eyes was worse, much worse. A girl could drown in those blue eyes with their ink-black pupils. Pupils that were flaring like spreading black pools just as I assumed mine were doing.

'How about you answer this question instead?' His voice was low and deep, his eyes with their flecks of blue and grey mesmerising. 'Would you *like* me to kiss you?'

Okay, so maybe I overstated my skill at lying a little bit. There was no way I could say 'no' and sound convincing. I was caught between a rock and a hard place. Me being the rock and Grayson being the hard place. He was standing so close I could just about feel his hard place. I was imagining it thrusting into me with vigorous energy. God, how I wanted to feel him deep inside. What was wrong with me? I am not the sort of girl to jump the bones of men I barely know, and especially men I don't even like. Especially men I'm not supposed to like because his grandfather ripped off my poor dead father.

'What do you think?' I asked instead, insanely proud of myself for evading a direct answer.

Grayson moved a couple of centimetres closer. I could smell his aftershave, and I had to stop myself from swaying towards him to breathe in more of that intoxicating scent. He lifted his hand to one of my dangly earrings and ever so gently toyed with it, running it over his finger. He didn't touch me at all, only my earring, but a riot of tingling sensations flooded my entire being.

'I think it would be crazy for us to go there.' His voice was so low and husky it sent a shiver across my skin.

'Go where?'

'Anywhere that involved touching each other.'

I could safely say I had never wanted a man to touch me more. It was ridiculous because I had once been engaged to be married and yet I had never fancied my ex as I fancied Grayson.

'You're touching my earring.' I injected a touch of asperity to my voice to disguise my wayward drives and urges.

His hand fell away from my earring and he gave a lopsided smile. 'My self-control had a moment.'

My self-control was having a moment too. A big moment. A moment I wasn't sure I could handle without a block and tackle or other industrial equipment. How was I going to keep my hands off Grayson Barlowe? Especially when he smiled in that self-deprecating way? I gave a stiff no-teeth-showing smile and stepped back but I could still feel the magnetic force of him.

'So, what are we going to do?' I glanced at my watch and winced at the time. 'It's getting late. We can hardly barge into Ethan and Niamh's room at this time of night. They might be…be…asleep.' There was no way I was going to say anything remotely sexual.

Grayson ran a hand through his hair and sighed. 'You're right. We'll arrange to meet them for breakfast instead.'

'We?'

'We have to be united on this, Ash.' It was the first time I had heard him say my preferred name and it sent a skittering shiver down my spine. When he had been talking to his mother, he had used my full name. At various conferences and awards nights in the past he had always been more formal, addressing me as Ms Clancy. Him using my shortened name made me feel as if we had crossed an invisible boundary line. A line I wasn't sure could be uncrossed so easily in the future.

Besides, he had touched my earring. That was big. Not my earring, but you know what I mean.

'I am absolutely with you on this,' I said. 'I can't bear the thought of Niamh making a huge mistake. Marriage is a big deal, it's not something anyone should rush into without careful consideration.'

'I couldn't agree more,' he said. 'Look, I think it's best if we arrive together tomorrow. I'll pick you up at half-six.'

*Half-six?*

'Just as well I'm a morning person.'

'I'm an early riser too.'

I was almost certain there was a double entendre to his statement but I was determined to ignore it. He'd said we were not going to touch. I agreed with it…sort of. Although my mind had already run wild with images of him rising early, his gloriously naked body unfolding itself from his million-thread snowy white bed linen that contrasted brilliantly with his deep tan. Yikes, be still my pulse…well, slow down a little at least.

'Where do you live? Oh, and you'd better give me your phone number in case we need to communicate,' Grayson said, taking out his phone again.

I rattled off my details and watched as he entered them in his phone with his two strong thumbs moving over the keys with such rapidity it made my single finger pecking look infantile. He pinged me a text and I then had his number. I felt a strange sense of accomplishment at having it in my possession. I was probably never going to be on his speed dial, nor he on mine, but still. At least I could contact him in an emergency.

On the way back to our cars a short time later, we walked shoulder to shoulder in the cool night air. It had finally stopped raining and the air smelt of summer stocks and jasmine and damp earth. The moon had peeped out from behind the clouds, casting a silvery glow over the wet pavement.

'What will you do if Ethan doesn't answer your text?' I asked. 'I haven't been able to contact Niamh. I think she's turned off her phone.'

'I got a reply from him when you went to the bathroom just then.'

Okay, so I didn't really need to take a leak, but I did want to peek at the penthouse bathroom. I wasn't disappointed. It was stunningly appointed with brass and Italian marble with ideal configurations for someone with limited mobility.

'Oh, what did he say? Is Niamh with him? Is she all right?'

'They're both fine and they've agreed to have breakfast with us,' he said, stopping as he got to my car.

'Well, that is good news.' I unlocked my car but before I could open the driver's door Gray-

son's hand moved past my body to do it for me.
'Oh, thank you…' I know I should have got in the
car and shut the door but I stayed where I was—
in the space between the open door and his strong
tall body. I slowly brought my gaze up to meet his
and my stomach did a complicated somersault that
would have scored a perfect ten at a gymnastics
event.

Our eyes locked. My mouth went dry. My heart
rate soared. A car horn bleated, jarring me out of
my stasis. 'Gosh, that was loud.'

'Yes, it was.' Grayson looked down into my
upturned face, his eyes moving between each of
mine before flicking to my mouth. I couldn't stop
staring at his mouth and the rich dark stubble that
surrounded it. I wondered what it would feel like
against my skin. I had to curl my fingers into my
palms to stop myself from lifting them to his face
to find out.

'Erm, so half-six then, right?' I sounded like a
nervous teenager agreeing to her first date with
the high school heartthrob.

His eyes were still on my mouth. 'Yep.'

I let out a shaky breath and stretched my lips
into one of my tight no-teeth-showing smiles.
'Well, goodnight.'

''Night.' He stepped back and I did a pretty
ungainly job of getting myself into my seat. I admire the royals and celebrities who have mastered

the art of entering and exiting a car with such elegant grace.

Grayson closed my door and stood back and watched me do an even worse job of getting out of the tight parking space. I stalled the car and ground the gears and gritted my teeth until my jaw clicked. I caught a glimpse of him in the rear-view mirror, still looking at me inscrutably as I drove off.

I tried to go to sleep as soon as I scrubbed off my make-up and brushed out my hair and flossed and cleaned my teeth. I counted sheep and cows and chickens to no avail. I was too wired for sleep. Too wound up with desire for a man I knew I should keep well away from. I don't do playboys. I don't do one-night stands. I don't do mortal enemies. But then, since I broke up with my ex, I haven't done anyone. Maybe my long period of celibacy was why I was reacting to Grayson in such an out of character way.

But I must have finally drifted off because when I woke it was six-fifteen. I sat bolt upright in my bed, my eyes still gritty from my poor night of sleep, my hair in such a tangle it made a rat's nest look neatly coiffed. I swore and threw off the bedcovers and rushed to the shower. There wasn't time to wash and blow-dry my hair, so I put on a shower cap instead.

With four and a half minutes to spare, I checked

myself in my full-length mirror. My dark brown hair was pulled back from my face in a smooth tight chignon at the back of my head. I was wearing white jeans with a silk shirt in a smoky grey. My make-up was understated but I'd highlighted my eyebrows with a kohl pencil, swiping a bit on my eyelids as well. I put on another pair of dangly earrings—I have lots of them in my jewellery kit. I have a skinny heart-shaped face so dangling earrings work well on me. Well, that's my story and I'm sticking to it.

I painted some lip-gloss on my lips and slipped my feet into a pair of high heels. I grabbed a jacket but from the look of the bright sky outside I probably wouldn't need it.

The doorbell rang and my heart leapt to my throat. I drew in a calming breath and walked to the door to check the security camera panel. Grayson looked disgustingly refreshed, as if he had slept as soon as his head landed on his feather pillow, although his hair was still damp. He had shaved too, highlighting the chiselled planes of his lean jaw.

I pressed the intercom. 'I'll be down in a tick.'

'No problem.'

I wanted to ask him up but I knew that was asking for trouble. The sort of trouble I wanted to stay away from, especially this early in the morning when I was tired and not in full working order. I needed a double shot of caffeine. And fast.

To my utmost surprise, Grayson had two takeaway coffees waiting in the car. The delicious aroma swirled around my nostrils and my mouth watered. I put on my seatbelt and glanced at him once he was behind the wheel. 'Is one of these for me?'

'Yep.'

I cocked my head at a suspicious angle. 'How do you know how I take it?'

A ghost of a smile flirted with his mouth. 'I took a guess. Long black, double shot, no sugar. Am I right?'

He was right, but I didn't want him to be. I needed to keep my distance and how was I to do that when he did thoughtful things like bring me coffee first thing in the morning?

'Yes.' I reached for the coffee and breathed in its delicious aroma, then took a sip. It didn't surprise me that the quality of the coffee was excellent. I had always known Grayson Barlowe had high standards—his body of award-winning work attested to that. The way he dressed, even when dressed casually as he was this morning, spoke of a man who valued quality.

I flicked my gaze his way again. 'But seriously, how did you know how I have my coffee? Do you have special mind-reading powers or something?'

His smile tilted one side of his mouth, making him look less serious and forbidding. His more relaxed features made my heart pitter-patter and my pulse race, as if I had downed the whole coffee in one swallow. And chased it with a couple of energy drinks.

'I overheard you order one at the design conference in Bristol last year.'

I gave him an arch look. 'I'm surprised you even noticed me. I seem to remember you were busy during the coffee and lunch breaks with a flock of young female architects who wanted to take a selfie with you.'

Ack. Why had I revealed that I had even noticed him with his entourage of adoring women? It made me look like I'd been following his every move at that wretched conference. The fact that I had was only because he was hard to ignore, even in a crowd. He was always head and shoulders over everyone else and had an arresting and commanding presence that drew my eye from way across a room.

Grayson gave me an inscrutable sideways glance and I could feel my cheeks heating under his scrutiny. 'You're hard to ignore.'

'Why's that?' I do not flirt. I do not fish for compliments. So it was kind of weird and out of character to hear myself ask such a flirty question.

He turned a corner at a busy junction and I

watched his broad-spanned hands control the steering wheel with competence and skill. I tried not to think of those hands competently and skilfully caressing my body. Tried but failed. I took another sip of my coffee, hoping it would redirect my wayward thoughts. It didn't.

Grayson focused his attention on the traffic in front of us. 'You're dedicated, hard-working and talented.'

'And that makes me stand out in a crowd?'

A fleeting smile traversed his lips. 'I could list all your other assets but that would be crossing a line we said we weren't going to cross.'

'You only said we weren't going to touch.' My gaze drifted to his muscular thigh so close to mine. I could have reached out and touched him right then and there. I wanted to but somehow I resisted the urge. Maybe my self-control wasn't as out of shape as I thought. Go me.

He drove the car into the valet parking bay at the hotel, then turned to look at me. 'So I did.' One of his hands was still on the steering wheel, the other grasping the gear stick. Was it my imagination or was he holding them a little *too* tightly, as if he was trying to stop himself from touching me? His gaze went to my mouth and I held my breath. I held it for so long I thought I might faint. Or maybe that was because his eyes were so sexily hooded and his mouth so gorgeously sculpted

I could think of nothing else but how it would feel pressed to mine.

I let out my breath in a shuddering stream. I licked my lips. I stared at his mouth, then flicked my gaze to meet his. 'You haven't changed your mind, have you?' I asked.

'It takes a lot to get me to change my mind.'

I twisted my mouth in a wry fashion. 'You sound a bit like me. Niamh is always calling me stubborn.'

He looked at me for another long moment without speaking, his eyes moving back and forth between each of mine, then over my face as if memorising my features. The curve of my cheeks, the arch of my eyebrows, the ski slope of my nose, the shape of my mouth.

'Stubbornness can be a weakness but it can also be a strength.'

'How so?'

'Someone who is stubborn is usually someone who stands by their convictions. They're steady and reliable.'

'Yes, well, I wish I'd been a bit more reliable twenty years ago,' I said before I could stop myself.

Grayson frowned. 'What happened twenty years ago?'

I bit my lip, wishing I hadn't let my guard down. I can't remember the last time I told anyone about the playground incident. I hate talking about it. I hate being reminded of how I ruined my sister's life. I glanced at the clock on the dashboard. We had ten minutes to spare, but I didn't want to be tempted to tell him my deepest darkest secret.

'Shouldn't we be going in? Ethan and Niamh might disappear again if we don't show up on time.'

'We've got plenty of time.' Grayson placed his hand on mine, where it was resting on my right thigh, and a jolt of energy coursed through my flesh.

I looked at his hand, his fingers so long and thick and tanned compared to mine.

'You're breaking the rules.' I tried to make my voice sound schoolmistressy, prim and proper. However, it came out kind of husky and breathless instead. But I didn't pull my hand out from under his. I couldn't. I liked the feel of his hand's warmth seeping into mine, the gentle squeeze of his fingers sending my heart rate off the charts. He had never touched me before, apart from toying with my dangly earring. This was so much better than that. His hand sent heat racing through my blood like tongues of flame.

Grayson slowly lifted his hand off mine, his mouth twisting in a rueful manner. 'Sorry. My bad.'

'It's okay.'

There was a beat or two of silence.

'I guess we'd better go in and get this over with,' he said, blowing out a breath of resignation.

'I can't say I'm looking forward to bursting their bubble.'

'But it has to be done. Ethan can't get married to a woman he has only known six weeks. I won't allow it.' The gritty determination was back in his tone, reminding me he was not going to change his mind in a hurry.

'Does he need your permission to marry? I mean, I know you're his custodian but he's an adult.'

'No, but I control the bulk of his trust fund.'

'Will you?' I asked, with a querying arch of my eyebrows.

'Will I what?'

'Make things difficult financially?'

A pleated frown pulled at his forehead. 'Not unless I have to.'

'So I guess Shakespeare was right in *A Midsummer Night's Dream*,' I said. '*"The course of true love never did run smooth."* You do realise by discouraging them it might backfire? Sometimes when we prohibit someone from doing something, the desire to do it is all the more fervent.' I was definitely speaking from experience—recent experience. I had a fervent desire to touch Grayson Barlowe and I didn't know how to quell it.

His eyes flicked to my mouth and back to my

gaze, but his expression was mask-like. 'That's a risk I'm prepared to take.'

I followed him into the hotel a short time later, wondering if I was prepared to risk spending time with him in the quest to put the brakes on my sister's relationship with his brother. It was dangerous being around Grayson Barlowe. Dangerous and exciting and thrilling. I rubbed my left hand over my right where the skin was still tingling from his touch. He had set the boundaries down but I wondered if that was for his benefit rather than mine. Or was I being a fanciful fool for thinking he might be remotely interested in someone like me?

# CHAPTER FOUR

GRAYSON GOT A security pass from reception to gain access to the lift that went to the floor where his brother and my sister were staying. His expression was grim as he came back to me with the security pass. 'They're in the honeymoon suite.'

The honeymoon suite? I chewed at my lower lip, wondering if Niamh and Ethan had consummated their relationship. Niamh knew the mechanics of sex because I had talked to her about consent and bodily autonomy even before she hit puberty. But she had never had a boyfriend before Ethan. I wondered if she was adequately prepared to deal with Ethan's physical limitations. But perhaps they were waiting until they got married. After all, six weeks wasn't a long time to wait. Maybe that's why they had decided on a short engagement. But…*the honeymoon suite?*

We got in the lift and Grayson swiped the pass

over the keypad and pressed the floor to the appropriate floor.

'Are you okay?' he asked with a deep note of concern in his voice.

I hadn't realised I was frowning, and I tried to straighten out the creases on my forehead. Unfortunately, I could do nothing about the hot colour I could feel pooling in my cheeks. 'My sister hasn't had a boyfriend before, so...'

'I'm sure Ethan would've been sensitive and put her needs ahead of his own.' His tone was calmly reassuring.

I disguised a swallow, feeling a fool for being so embarrassed at discussing our siblings' sex life with him. Seriously, I was behaving like an innocent Regency heroine instead of a twenty-first century career woman who'd once been engaged to be married. 'That's...erm...good to hear.'

'Ethan is a partial paraplegic in that he can still walk a few steps.'

I wasn't sure why he was filling me in on that detail, other than to assure me his brother was not as disabled as I had first thought.

'I didn't know that.'

'He had a stroke following the accident. A brain bleed took out his right side, but he worked hard at rehab and got a bit more movement, apart from his right hand.'

We arrived on the honeymoon suite floor and

the lift opened with a whooshing sound. We stepped out of the lift but by tactic agreement stood in the wide corridor while the doors closed again behind us on another whisper.

'It must have been a harrowing time for you both, and, of course, your parents.'

A shadow passed over his features like clouds scudding across the sky. 'We could so easily have lost him. It still gives me nightmares about how close it was.' The gravity in his voice reminded me of my own visits to the ICU where Niamh was hooked up to a ventilator for weeks on end. The uncertainty was torture, each day unfolding with a new hurdle, a new drama to face. Then a flicker or two of hope, only to be dashed the following day.

'I understand. I know lots of people say that, but how can they if they haven't stood by a loved one's bedside, wondering if they would be alive the next day?'

Grayson's eyes held mine and I found myself unable to look away. 'What happened to your sister?'

I let out a ragged sigh. 'A head injury when she was seven. She fell off a swing and fractured her skull. She was in a coma for a month. When she finally woke up, she had no memory of the accident. No idea of how close we were to losing her.' I swallowed tightly and added, 'It was my fault.'

He frowned. 'How was it your fault?'

'I was supposed to be watching her.'

'How old were you?'

'Nine.'

'Isn't that a bit young to be responsible for a small child? Where were your parents?'

I let out another rough-edged sigh, wondering why I was unloading all this emotional drama to my sworn enemy. 'My dad had died two years before. My mother was still struggling to cope, so I used to take Niamh to the park after school to give Mum a break.'

Grayson's frown was still deeply entrenched on his forehead. It gave him a severe and intimidating appearance, but when I looked into his eyes I could see a blue ocean that wasn't cold and icy at all. There were warm currents swirling in the depths.

'And all these years you've been blaming yourself?'

I shrugged one shoulder. 'Who else is there to blame? I was supposed to be watching out for her and I turned away to look at something, I can't even remember what it was now. I heard a scream and turned back to see Niamh on the ground, bleeding from her head and ears. It wasn't Niamh who'd screamed but another child who saw it happen. Fortunately, there were a couple of people nearby walking their dogs and they called an ambulance.'

'I'm sorry you and Niamh had such a terrible

thing happen, but you really mustn't blame yourself, Ash.'

'How can I not? I changed the course of her life that day. Her potential was stolen by my inattention.'

Grayson placed one of his hands on my shoulder and a shudder of awareness coursed through my body. His touch was warm, anchoring, stabilising. Grounding me in a way I had not felt before. Our eyes met and, in that moment, I sensed that here was someone who truly understood the emotional trauma of watching someone they love hover between life and death.

'I blame myself too for my brother's accident. It was a snap decision to swap seats that night. He hadn't had much experience driving in the rain and yet I agreed to let him take over the wheel. It was the worst decision of my life.'

I placed my hand over his where it was resting on my shoulder. I could feel the soft dark hairs on the back of his hand against my palm and fingers. I could see the anguish and guilt in his eyes that reminded me so much of my own. I gave his hand a gentle squeeze, marvelling at how broad his hand was compared to mine.

'I'm guessing you don't make snap decisions any more, right?'

His mouth twisted ruefully, and he lifted his

hand away from my shoulder, taking my hand with it. 'Not usually.'

His thumb stroked over the back of my hand in a slow-motion caress that sent searing heat coursing through my flesh. His touch was so light, tender almost, and it should not have caused the riot of sensations in my body, but somehow it did and I—shame on me—did nothing to stop it.

Only the sound of the honeymoon suite door opening finally made me pull my hand out of Grayson's light hold. I turned to face my sister, who was dressed in smart casual clothes, her hair brushed and tied in a neat ponytail.

'You're late,' Niamh said, eyeballing me.

'Only five minutes or so,' I said, glancing at my watch.

She gave Grayson a hard stare and then turned and led the way inside the honeymoon suite. We followed her without a word and then Grayson closed the door, exchanging a brief raised brow glance with me that made something turn over in my belly. We walked to the sitting room off the foyer of the suite, where Ethan was seated on a plush sofa rather than in his wheelchair. His expression matched Niamh's defiant you-can't-tell-me-how-to-live-my-life look.

'I hope you both realise the stress you caused us both last night by disappearing without telling us where you were going,' Grayson said in a stern tone that I knew was not going to work with my sister. And, judging from Ethan's expression, it wasn't going to work with him either.

Niamh sat beside Ethan and grasped his hand. 'Your reaction to our announcement was so upsetting.' Tears shone in her eyes, and she continued with a wobble in her voice, 'I thought you'd be happy for us and instead you tried to ruin what was supposed to be one of the most memorable days of our lives.'

Ethan seemed to grow a few centimetres as he held his older brother's gaze. 'I brought Niamh here to c-compensate for her disappointment in how you b-both reacted to our news.'

'Look, I'm sorry about that,' I said before Grayson could respond. 'But it was such a surprise to drop on us. We didn't even know you were seeing each other.' It felt kind of weird to be saying 'we' all the time as if Grayson and I were a couple.

Niamh met my gaze with her watery one. 'Is it because of what happened to Daddy all those years ago?' Her question was directed at both of us—me and Grayson.

'No,' Grayson answered.

'Yes,' I answered at the same time.

Grayson locked his gaze on mine, one of his dark eyebrows rising in an arc. 'Seriously?'

I straightened my shoulders and held his querying look. 'Our father would still be alive today if it hadn't been for your grandfather ripping him off in that so-called friendly merger. Any merger between the Clancys and Barlowes is to be discouraged, even romantic ones.'

Especially romantic ones that involved Grayson and me, but of course I didn't say that out loud.

A ripple of tension passed over Grayson's features and his mouth went into a straight line. 'I wondered when you were going to bring that old chestnut up.' His tone was ripe with derision. 'But perhaps you should get your facts straight before you start maligning my late grandfather.'

I gave him stare for stare, my blood pounding with anger. 'The facts are your grandfather reneged on the deal at the last minute and left my father practically penniless.'

The arch of his eyebrow went higher. 'Is that what you were told?'

A sliver of doubt got under the door of my dislike of all things Barlowe. It shone a tiny light on my beliefs and made me wonder if I had been told the truth or what my mother wanted me to believe. I had idolised my father and I had only been seven years old when he died. Details about business mergers were not exactly things I was interested in as a small child. I seemed to recall My Little Pony was front and centre back then. Could I have got it wrong about him? But why then did people in the architectural community still refer to Grayson's grandfather as a hard man who didn't suffer fools gladly?

But then another thought slipped into my head... What if my father had been foolish in some way?

Grayson must have seen the doubts flickering over my face for he turned and addressed his brother and my sister again. I was incredibly grateful for the subject change, but I dearly wanted to unpick the past with him on some other occasion, preferably when we were alone.

'Whatever happened in the past has no bearing on what's happening now. You both want to be together; Ash and I are not in any doubt of that. But we want you to slow down a bit before you take the next step.'

'What t-t-time frame are you suggesting?' Ethan asked with a wary expression.

'Six months,' Grayson said.

'Three,' I said. I didn't want to look like I agreed with him on every detail.

The young couple exchanged glances and then Ethan said, 'One m-month and th-that's our final answer.'

I was secretly proud of Niamh's defiant stare aimed at Grayson and me. And more than a little envious of Ethan's proud glance at her and his warm, encouraging smile.

'Okay, so here's the deal,' Grayson said. 'In one

month's time, we'll regroup and assess how things are going. If you still want to be together, we can talk about what comes next.'

Ethan's expression became guarded again. 'Will you promise to support us in our goal of getting married?'

Grayson's jaw worked for a moment. 'Why can't you just live together to see if you're compatible in the medium to long term?'

I folded my arms across my chest and gave Grayson a raised brow look. 'My, oh, my, you really do have a phobia about marriage, don't you?' I have to say, I rather enjoyed needling him a bit. It was only fair since he made my heart go pitter-patter and my belly flip-flop, and my common sense to go offline.

'I have nothing against marriage between the right people,' Grayson said.

'You don't think we're the right people?' Niamh's eyes shimmered with a fresh tide of tears. 'I know I'm not smart like you and Ash, but I love Ethan and I will do everything in my power to be a wonderful wife and companion to him.'

Grayson looked a little uncomfortable in the face of my sister's emotional outburst…or was he uncomfortable about her level of disability? Did he doubt she could be a loving wife and companion to his brother? Or did he still think she was a gold-digger, after his brother's trust fund? After all,

Grayson controlled the bulk of Ethan's finances. There could not be a wedding without his say-so, or at least not the sort of wedding my sister had dreamed of since she was a kid. No Elvis impersonators for her. Niamh wanted one of those big meringue-like dresses with a long train and veil, and a church full of flowers and a choir, not a ten-minute ceremony in some dinky little chapel in Vegas.

Grayson let out a long breath. 'Let's see how things pan out after a month.'

'Will you promise to be s-supportive and open to us being t-together in the meantime?' Ethan asked.

'Yes,' I said, mentally crossing my fingers because I still had my doubts about how a marriage between them would work. I did so much day-to-day stuff for Niamh. How was Ethan going to help her when he had his own needs to consider? But then I reminded myself—he could love her and that was what she wanted more than anything.

'There's one other thing…' Ethan added, grasping Niamh's hand again. 'We want you both to design a house for us. One that will suit both our needs perfectly.'

'Both of us?' I asked in alarm. I could not imagine working alongside Grayson Barlowe…well, not without being tempted to cross the boundary between professional and personal. It would mean spending even more time with him. Lengthy periods of time. Designing a house was not a weekend project. Some houses took weeks, if not months, to design according to the client's specifications.

'You're both award-winning architects,' Niamh said. 'We thought it would show your support of our relationship by designing our dream home for us.'

Grayson looked at me but his expression was as hard to read as a slab of marble. He turned back to eyeball his younger brother. 'What's wrong with your penthouse? It suits your needs, doesn't it?'

'It's a penthouse,' Ethan said as if that explained everything. 'Niamh and I want a house and garden. And we want to live in the country, not in the city.'

Grayson's jaw worked for a moment, which suggested to me his brain was filing through the arguments against such a move, but in the end he didn't say anything. He merely shrugged one broad shoulder and turned to answer a knock at the door.

Breakfast was delivered to the room at that point, but I didn't have much appetite. I picked at a croissant and had half a cup of coffee and watched as Grayson had even less. Ethan and Niamh tucked in, however, and Ethan seemed delighted with the enjoyment my sister was having in indulging in the delicious options on the trolley. Eggs Benedict, an artfully displayed fruit platter, little pots of yoghurt in various flavours, pastries and croissants with preserves, tea and coffee and freshly squeezed orange juice. It was a breakfast junkie's heaven, but I could feel myself sinking into a private hell of despair.

A house in the country? Co-designed by Grayson and me? How would my sister cope without me? We had lived together all our lives. My whole life revolved around her and work. I wasn't used to thinking only of myself. How would I fill the hours and days and weeks and months and years? And, more to the point, how would Niamh handle marriage to a man who needed so much help himself? The architectural project aside, if she married Ethan, Grayson would be her brother-in-law and it would not be so easy for me to avoid him. And I needed to avoid him, otherwise I was going to be in water deep enough to cloud my vision all over again.

Half an hour later, Grayson and I left the honeymoon suite and got back in the lift. The doors whooshed closed, and I met his gaze. 'So, that was a bit unexpected.'

His eyes glinted with cynicism. 'You think?'

I gave a shrug and toyed with the strap of my tote bag with my fingers. 'Well, at least they've promised not to get married for a month. That's a positive, right?'

One of his hands opened and closed, the other

scraped a rough pathway through his thick hair. 'I hope a month is long enough for them to see the stupidity of getting married at all. And as to a house in the country,' he muttered a curse swear word and continued, 'that's even more preposterous.'

I cocked my head on one side and studied him for a beat or two. Unlike me, he didn't seem too fazed by my unwavering scrutiny. 'Are you worried about working with me on their house?'

A tiny muscle flickered near his mouth. 'I've done collaborative work before.'

'You didn't answer my question.'

'No, I'm not the least bit worried.' He enunciated each word as if speaking to a child. 'Are you?'

I twisted my mouth. 'It depends.'

'On what?'

'Whether we can work together without arguing over every light switch placement.'

'It won't be a problem.' His tone seemed to suggest otherwise, so too did the taut line of his mouth and the flicker of annoyance in his gaze.

'Back there, you said marriage between the right people was okay.' I raised my fingers in air quotes and said with a challenging note in my voice, 'Define the right people.'

The lift doors opened on the foyer level and Grayson silently indicated for me to precede him. We walked along the marbled area for some distance before he spoke. 'Marriage can work reasonably well between two mature adults who have insight into their own psychodynamics.'

'You don't think your brother is mature enough for marriage?'

He gave me a sideways glance. 'Is your sister?'

My shoulders went down on a sigh. 'In some ways, yes, in others, no.' I stopped walking to look up at him. 'There's something I want to discuss with you. In private.'

He stopped in his tracks, his eyebrows lifting ever so slightly, and a glint came into his eyes. 'Oh?'

'It's about the feud between your grandfather and my father.'

The glint hardened to flint, and he resumed walking. 'It's in the past, it's best left there.'

I trotted to keep up with him and placed my hand on his muscled forearm to get him to stop. He stopped and glanced at my hand on his arm before meeting my gaze.

'I thought we agreed not to touch?' he said with a sardonic quirk of his lips that made me want to touch him even more.

I took my hand off his arm and let it drop by my side. 'I want to know more about what happened between your grandfather and my father. There seems to be some discrepancy between what I've been told by my mother and what you understand to be true.'

'Are you free for dinner tonight?'

The question utterly blindsided me. I stood there with my mouth hanging open, unable to get my voice to work. Finally, I managed to croak in an incredulous tone, 'Dinner?'

'You're clearly not a fan of breakfast, so I thought dinner might be more suitable.'

So he had noticed my lack of appetite at breakfast. Interesting.

'I normally love breakfast but...' I chewed at my lower lip for a moment. 'Dinner as in a...?'

'It's not a date.' His tone was emphatic, annoyingly so. 'Call it a history lesson if you like.'

'A history lesson?' I knew I was parroting him but I couldn't get my head around spending more time alone with him—at his request. But I did want to hear his side of things about the leadup to my father's suicide.

'Okay. When and where?'

'My place.'

I frowned. 'Your place? Why not a restaurant?'

'You said you wanted our discussion to be private.'

'Right, well... Do you want me to bring anything?'

'No. And I'll pick you up.'

I was privately impressed by his chivalrous offer, but I didn't want to communicate it to him.

'Why? I'm perfectly able to get myself to your place.'

'I know, but I'd prefer to pick you up.'

'Is that so you can control when it's time for me to leave?'

He gave a ghost of a smile. 'I promise not to keep you long.'

Given he was a sleep-with-them-and-leave-them playboy, I could only imagine the ridiculously short timeframe on his relationships. I gave him a pert look. 'I bet you say that to all the girls.'

He threw his head back and laughed and I was totally blindsided again. I had never heard him laugh before. He had a deep rich laugh that made the fine hairs on my arms stand up at the roots. I wanted to hear more of it. I wanted to see his face relax in humour rather than tense up in stern disapproval. He was a stop-your-pulse-handsome man either way, but when he laughed it completely transformed him. It gave me a glimpse of who he had been before his brother's accident—a happy-go-lucky man who had no reason to frown.

'Shall we say eight p.m.?' he said, with a smile still curving his mouth.

'Fine. Eight it is.'

Seriously, if he had said two in the morning, I would still have said yes.

# CHAPTER FIVE

MY WORK DAYS normally flash past but this day was as slow as a snail on crutches. I had trouble giving my clients my full attention. My brain kept drifting off to what I might wear for my dinner with Grayson. I mentally examined the contents of my wardrobe and decided I needed to hit the high street in my lunch hour. *Lunch hour, ha-ha.* I *never* took a lunch hour. I normally worked through because there wasn't enough time in the day with all I had to do for Niamh as well as work. But since she was still with Ethan, presumably at his penthouse apartment by now, I had more time on my hands.

After forty-five minutes of trying on clothes in various boutiques, I concluded I was a terrible shopper. I couldn't decide what to buy for my non-date dinner with Grayson. There was a part of me that wanted to wow him. I might not be super-model material, but I can really rock a little black dress and sky-high heels. But another part of me wanted to keep things casual. I didn't want him to think I was hitting on him, especially since he was the one who'd orchestrated the no-touching rule. The rule I was having so much trouble sticking to.

In the end, I went for the little black dress. A new and ridiculously expensive one because I didn't want to wear anything I had worn before. Clothes can be as evocative as music. I got rid of a lot of my clothes when I ended my relationship with my ex. Most of my wardrobe represented my failure to see our relationship for what it was. And the one thing in life I try my best to avoid is failure.

It was bang on eight p.m. when my doorbell rang. I gave myself a quick glance in the full-length mirror in my bedroom. My hair was up in a bun that took me *ages* to appear makeshift and casual. My make-up was impeccable, my perfume subtle but fragrant. I wore my favourite dangly earrings—they were so dangly they almost brushed my shoulders and tinkled when I moved. My dress was worth every penny. It clung to my body in all the right places, making me feel feminine and attractive in a way I had not felt before. Or maybe that's what spending heaps of money on a dress does to you—it makes you want to believe it was worth it.

I opened the front door a short time later to see Grayson standing there looking handsome enough to stop my heart. My breath stalled, and my pulse went a little haywire. He was wearing a light blue blazer teamed with trousers in a navy blue and his shirt was white, highlighting his tanned complexion. His jaw was clean-shaven and his hair still damp from a shower, and I could smell his aftershave, an alluring mix of citrus and wood and country leather.

'Hi,' I said. 'I'll just get my purse and phone.'

He waited politely outside, which impressed me. Seems I wasn't the only one big on manners. I came back to him with purse and phone in hand and a stiff smile on my face.

'How was your day?' I asked.

'Busy. How was yours?'

'Long.'

He stood there looking at me for a long moment. I smoothed my free hand down the side of my dress. 'Is something wrong?'

He rapid-blinked and smiled lopsidedly. 'You look very beautiful in that dress.'

'Oh, this old thing?' See? I am hopeless at accepting compliments. Not that many come my way, but still.

Grayson's smile informed me I hadn't fooled him one iota. For a moment I thought I might have left the price tag on, but no, I recalled I had snipped it off with some scissors.

'Love the earrings.'

I lifted my hand to toy with one. 'A client made them for me. They're my favourite pair. I only wear them on special occasions.' I suddenly realised what I'd just said and clamped my lips shut, furious for letting slip how much I was looking forward to this evening with him. I could feel my cheeks heating enough to put the sun out of a job. 'I—I mean, not that this evening is anything special, it's just I haven't been out in a while. I'm usually so busy with Niamh and work and stuff...' I grimaced at the way I was running off at the mouth like a gauche teenager.

Grayson lifted his hand from by his side and gently flicked my left earring with his finger, the soft tinkling sound in the silence as loud as a gong. 'Are you nervous about having dinner with me?'

'No.' I could feel my blush deepening as if someone had turned up the thermostat in my body. My breathing was a little erratic, my pulse racing. 'Why would I be nervous?'

His hand went back to his side. 'You're entering enemy territory.'

'I—I am?'

His crooked smile tilted a little further. 'That's how you see me, isn't it? As the enemy?'

'Well, we're not exactly friends. We're business rivals.'

'The two aren't mutually exclusive.'

Somehow, I couldn't envisage him being a close

friend to me. I had no doubt he would make a good one, but I needed to keep my distance.

'I have enough friends.' Not quite true. I lost a few friends when I broke up with my ex. People always take sides in messy breakups. And with my caring responsibilities with my mother and sister over the years, friends had often simply drifted away because I was so rarely available to hang out with them. I wouldn't describe myself as lonely, though. I am too self-sufficient for that. I have taught myself not to need people.

'You're never going to forgive me for winning that award, are you?'

I hated that he knew how much I had coveted that wretched award. It made me seem petty and childish, a sore loser.

'It wasn't that big a deal.'

'If it's any comfort, I think you should've won it.'

I looked up at him in surprise. 'Really?'

His expression was set in more serious lines. 'The McClean project was a difficult one and you handled it with a high level of creativity and skill.'

'But they gave the award to you.'

He shrugged one broad shoulder. 'You win some, you lose some. Awards don't mean much to me these days. They look good on the CV, but I don't need them to boost my ego. I know I'm good at what I do.'

I let out a tiny sigh. 'I envy your confidence…'

'You have no reason to doubt your ability.'

I gave a twist of a smile. 'That's two in the space of minutes.'

'Two what?'

'Compliments.'

His eyes held mine for a long interval. I found it impossible to look away. My heart was banging like a tribal drum, so too my pulse. I could feel its echo between my legs, an intimate beat that stirred my primal drives into restlessness.

'I could make it three, but you'd probably slap my face.' His voice was deep and husky, and it made my pulse race even more.

'Are you flirting with me?'

He gave another crooked smile. 'I'm trying not to, but you look good enough to eat in that dress. Speaking of eating—we'd better get going. I don't want the dinner I left cooking to set off the smoke alarm.'

I went with him to his car, which was parked outside my townhouse. I wasn't worried about his cooking setting off the fire alarm. My simmering body was probably going to do that all by itself.

Grayson pulled up in front of a gorgeous eighteen-forties mansion in Kensington and I had to stop myself from drooling. The five-storey house was white with a black wrought iron fence, which matched the iron lace of the long slim balcony that ran the width of the building on the second level. There were four topiary spheres in pots situated on the balcony and small lime-green neatly trimmed pines were in the front garden in a window box that jutted out from a window above the lowest level. Seriously, I was feeling like Elizabeth Bennet on first setting eyes on Pemberley in Jane Austen's *Pride and Prejudice*. Maybe I needed to rethink how much I disliked Grayson Barlowe... but *did* I dislike him?

My feelings were a little confused on that front. I wanted to dislike him. I wanted to keep him at a distance. I wanted to see him as my enemy because of the history between our families. But somehow it was becoming harder and harder to summon up that intense level of dislike. I had witnessed the care and concern he had for his brother. I had heard him laugh. I had felt his touch on my shoulder and my hand. And my earring. I could only imagine what it would feel like to have his lips press down on mine.

I pulled myself back into line. Kissing him was out of the question. It must *not* happen.

Because I was staring open-mouthed at his house for so long, I hadn't realised Grayson had exited the car and was now around my side, opening the door for me. I stepped out of the car with as much grace as I could muster, but my high

heels caught on something and I pitched forward.
I would have face planted on the footpath if he
hadn't caught me by the arm. His fingers gripped
me, and a shiver ran down my spine at the tensile
strength in his stabilising hold.

'Are you okay?'

'I'm fine… I think…'

He kept hold of me until I was safely on the
footpath. When his hand finally fell away from my
arm I surreptitiously ran my hand over where his
fingers had gripped me, and something in my belly
softly unfolded like a flower opening its petals.

He laid a hand lightly to my elbow as we walked
up the steps leading to the front door. I didn't object because, right then, I didn't think I was capable of walking unaided. My legs were feeling like
soggy noodles and my heart was still hammering
enough to send a cardiologist into a panic.

Grayson opened the front door, and I stepped
past him to enter the Italian marble entrance hall.
I swept my gaze over every angle, noting how the
light came in, the sweep of the grand staircase,
the priceless antiques and artworks that made the
mansion such a showcase of design and upmarket
taste without being too over the top.

'Nice digs,' I said.

'Thanks.'

'Have you lived here long?'

'Ten years.' Grayson closed the front door.

'Come through to the sitting room while I check on dinner.'

'Don't spoil my enjoyment of watching a man cook. Or did you get your housekeeper to rustle something up?'

He gave a rueful smile. 'My housekeeper is a terrible cook.'

'Then why do you keep her?'

'Him.'

I blinked in surprise. 'Him?'

'Romeo is great at cleaning and gardening, but he's got a way to go before I'll let him loose in the kitchen.'

'Romeo is Italian?'

'Yep, I met him when I was in Florence. He was looking for work, so I brought him home with me. He helps Ethan too. He lives downstairs but he's out tonight.'

I followed Grayson to the kitchen at the back of the house. 'So how old is he?'

'Nineteen but he's been here a couple of years now.'

'And his family were okay with him moving to London?'

Grayson pulled out a kitchen stool for me to sit on. 'He doesn't have any family, or at least none he wants to have anything to do with. He was home-less when I met him, begging for food.'

'Gosh, that's terrible. Poor kid. But great that

you stepped in. But you were taking a risk inviting a teenager you didn't know to come and live with you.'

'I'm a pretty good judge of character. Besides, doesn't everyone deserve a chance to prove themselves?'

'I guess…' Somehow, I hadn't pictured Grayson as the sort of man to take in a homeless kid. Or maybe I had always been so heavily biased against him, I hadn't seen the admirable qualities he possessed. I do my bit for charity, and I can't walk past a homeless person without giving them money or buying them food, but I had never considered inviting someone to live with me. But then, I had the care and safety of my sister to consider. Or at least I had until now.

Grayson opened a cupboard where glassware was kept. 'What would you like to drink? Wine? Champagne? G and T?'

'White wine would be lovely, thanks.'

He opened a bottle of French white wine and poured some into two glasses, handing me one across the wide bench. 'Here you go. Cheers.'

'Cheers.' I clinked my glass against his, but I wasn't sure exactly what we were toasting. 'So, do you do all your own cooking?'

'I eat out a fair bit.'

'Yes, well, of course you do, being a playboy and all.'

He frowned and put down his wineglass. 'You know, the press like to paint a certain picture of me that's not always accurate.'

I toyed with the stem of my wineglass. 'How long do your relationships last?'

'Not long.'

'Why?'

'Because I'm not interested in settling down.' He turned away to stir something on the hob. I studied his strong back and shoulders and had to stop myself drooling again. The food smelled amazing, but it was his physique that got my attention.

I took another sip of wine. 'But you can't deny you've had a lot of lovers.'

'There're no notches on my bedpost. You can check if you like.'

'I think it's best if I stay out of your bedroom, don't you?' Two sips of wine and I was tipsy. Or maybe it was his company that was making me lose my head.

He turned around and met my gaze and a hot tingle rolled down my back and fizzed like a firework at the base of my spine. 'You don't seem the type of woman to get involved with a playboy.' He glanced at my empty ring finger before returning his gaze to mine. 'Or do you crave a walk on the wild side now you've set yourself free?'

I could not tear my gaze away from his if I tried. But then I didn't try. I wanted to stare into that blue-grey gaze and totally lose myself. Lose my sensible, rational side and play with capital D danger. There was a powerful energy crackling between his gaze and mine, an energy I could feel travelling through my body like a high voltage current. His gaze drifted to my mouth, and I couldn't stop myself from sweeping the tip of my tongue over my lips.

'How wild are you?' Was that my voice? That husky femme fatale voice I had never heard come from my mouth before.

Grayson walked around to my side of the kitchen island bench. My heart rate ratcheted up with every slow and purposeful step he took towards me. He took the wineglass from my fingers and set it down in front of me with an audible clunk that sent a shockwave of lust through my body. He swung me up on the stool so I was face to face with him, his legs either side of mine, effectively caging me. He didn't touch me, but he was close enough to and that was enough to send my senses reeling. I craved his touch like a drug addict craves their next hit.

'I—I thought we weren't going to do this.' My voice was thready and breathless.

'What do you think I'm going to do?'

'Kiss me?' I framed it as a question, almost like a command, only realising my mistake when he glanced at my mouth again.

'Is that what you want me to do?' His voice went down another couple of semitones.

I moistened my lips and swallowed. 'I'm tempted.'

A gleam of satisfaction shone in his gaze. 'So, what are we going to do? Stick to the rules or get up close and personal?'

'You're pretty close right now.'

'I can get closer.' The gravel-rough edge to his tone sent a wave of scorching heat through my lower body. Grayson lifted his hand to my face, one of his fingers tracing the curve of my right cheek all the way down to the base of my chin. His touch was light and yet electric and every nerve in my face reacted.

I closed my eyes as he sent his finger on a slow exploration of my lips. I tried to hold back a whimper of pleasure but wasn't entirely successful. No one had ever touched me with such exquisite tenderness, with such slow deliberation. I had no way of handling it other than to enjoy it. My lips tingled with each faineant brush of his fingers, my breath stop-starting as I tried to control my reaction. I had never considered myself a particularly sensual person. I hadn't hated sex with my other partners, but I hadn't loved it either.

But I sensed I would love it with Grayson Barlowe.

He would make sure of it.

He tipped up my chin with one of his fingers

and I opened my eyes to find his gaze locked on mine. 'If we kiss, it's just a kiss, understood?'

'What? You think if we kiss I'll start sending out wedding invitations in the next post?'

He smiled at my attempt at humour. 'Don't even think about it. I have no plans to get married.'

'Nor do I.'

His hand came up to rest against the base of my neck. I had no idea my skin was so sensitive at my hairline, no idea how wonderful it felt to have a man's fingers splay into my hair. A shiver passed over my scalp like a Mexican wave and my insides coiled and tightened with sudden savage lust. His eyes lowered to my mouth and I held my breath, my heart beating so heavily I was sure he could feel it, let alone hear it. He brought up his other hand and traced a slow outline of my mouth with a lazy finger.

'You have a beautiful mouth.' His voice was low and deep and sexy, so sexy it made every millimetre of my skin lift in a shiver.

I couldn't take my own eyes off his mouth. The shape of it fascinated me, the sensually shaped contours making me ache to feel them moving against my lips. I lifted my hand to his face and traced his mouth as he had traced mine, another wave of lust rolling through me as the rasp of his stubble grazed my finger.

'You're not burning dinner, are you?' My voice

was barely above a whisper, my thumping heart-beat loud enough for the neighbours to hear.

Grayson gently tugged me off the stool so I was standing in front of him, close enough for our hips to meet. A bomb went off in my blood, an explosion of heat and fire that left no corner of my body unaffected. I yearned to move even closer, to press my pelvis harder against his, to feel the contour of his body rising against me. It was an urge, a primal drive I suddenly couldn't control. I placed my hands on his trim hips and leaned into him, a gasp escaping my lips as the heat from his hard body met mine.

His mouth came down and captured mine in a kiss that sent a shockwave of ferocious need through my flesh. I could feel the pulsing ache of my lower body, a secret ache that silently begged to be assuaged. His tongue demanded entry to my mouth and I opened to him on a breathless whimper of heady, blissful pleasure. Hot streaks of longing flashed through the core of my being, leaving fire trails in their wake. I was burning for him, on fire for the possession of his body.

Grayson shifted position to gain better access to my mouth, his lips hard and yet soft and utterly irresistible. His hands came up to cradle my face and I shivered from head to foot at the sheer magic of his touch. His tongue played with mine in a cat and mouse caper that sent my senses reeling and my pulse racing off the charts. It was a kiss of dominance and, God help me, I submitted to it. Totally. How could I not? I was becoming addicted to the flick and dart of his tongue; I was captivated by the firm exploration of his lips and the explosive energy that generated between us.

His hands moved from cradling my face to hold me by the hips. He pulled me closer to his body and I nearly came on the spot. He was hard. Rock-hard. So hard I could almost feel the thundering throb of his blood. He lifted his mouth off mine and looked down at me with his blue-grey eyes glinting with raw, earthy lust.

'I was so determined to keep my hands off you.' His tone had a generous hint of ruefulness and his mouth twisted. 'Like that was ever going to work.'

I lifted one of my hands to the back of his neck and played with the ends of his dark hair, my breasts pushing against his broad chest, my lower body humid and wet with want. 'You're proving rather irresistible as well.'

His eyes darkened as they held mine. 'If we were both sensible, we'd stop this right now before things get out of control.'

'Do you want to stop?' I could not believe how forward I was being. I'm no prude and I'm all for women owning their body's desires and needs, but practically begging Grayson to make love to me was a little out of character to say the least. He

was my enemy, my rival. I didn't even like him…
all that much.

But my body had other ideas. It liked him very
much indeed. It desired him like it had desired no
one else. It throbbed and ached and pulsed for his
touch. I thought I was possibly going to *die* if he
didn't kiss me again.

Grayson's hands tightened their hold on my hips
and a shiver coursed down my spine. 'If we do
this, it's only going to be once. To get it out of our
system, understood?' His tone was adamant but
something about the scorching heat in his gaze
made me wonder if he was saying it more for his
own benefit, not mine.

I raised my eyebrows in a playful manner.
'What if once isn't enough?'

'It will be.' He let out a short harsh-sounding
breath. 'It will have to be.'

'Because?'

'Because I have a rule about mixing business
with pleasure.'

I lowered my hand from playing with his hair
and laid it flat against his chest instead. His heart
was thumping hard underneath my palm and a frisson of delight rushed through me to think he was
as attracted to me as I was to him. The sense of
power it gave me went to my head. I straightened
his shirt collar and then gave his chest a dismis-
sive little pat and stepped back to put some dis-

tance between us. I had to before I was tempted to cross a line I hadn't crossed before.

'It's a good rule. But I have a rule as well.'

'What is it?' There was a guardedness about his expression—a slight narrowing of his gaze, a tensing of his features.

I locked my gaze on his, determined not to be the first to look away. 'I don't do one-night stands.'

One side of his mouth lifted in a cynical fashion, but I was sure I saw genuine regret in his eyes. 'Then it seems we're at an impasse.'

'Because you won't change your mind.' I framed it as a statement instead of a question.

Grayson closed the distance between us and then picked up a loose strand of my hair and wound it around his finger, tethering me to him in a deliciously scalp-tugging, skin-tingling way. 'Are we a case of immovable object meets unstoppable force?' His voice was lightly teasing but there was a deadly seriousness in his gaze.

'Could be.' Another shiver rolled down my spine as his finger wound a little tighter. He was stirring in me a wild and reckless want that threatened to get out of control.

He slowly bent his head and lowered his mouth to the edge of mine. His warm breath skated across my lips and my insides quaked with longing. 'What if we just do this then?' He brushed his lips against mine, sending volcanic heat straight to my core.

I tried to suppress a whimper of delight but didn't quite manage it. 'F-fine…' I shuddered as his lips touched down on mine again. A feather-light touch that was no less arousing than his firmer kiss earlier. My lips tingled for more contact and my body throbbed hard and fast and furiously with need.

'It's been a long time since I kissed someone without it going any further.' His lips went on an exquisite exploration of my right cheek, his tongue darting out to stroke my skin, making my legs all but fold beneath me. My bones were turning to liquid, my ligaments loosening, my muscles melting.

I clutched at the front of his shirt, my mouth so close to his I could feel the soft waft of his breath against my lips. 'The self-discipline will be good for you.' Even if it was proving torturous for me.

He grunted in wry agreement and then his lips went to the side of my neck, his stubble grazing my skin in a toe-curling manner. 'You smell amazing.' His voice was lower than I had ever heard it, low and husky as if it was coming from beneath the floorboards.

I tilted my head to one side, the feel of his lips moving against the skin of my neck sending flickers of delight through my body. My dangly earring tinkled as he stroked his tongue against the cartilage of my ear. How was I going to resist him when he kissed and caressed me so exquisitely? I had never been so worked up before. It was like there was a unique alchemy between us, a chemical, combustible reaction that sent shockwaves through my female flesh.

'Grayson?'

He straightened to look down at me, his hands resting on my hips. 'Time to stop?'

I didn't want to stop but I had to exhibit some measure of self-control. I wrinkled my nose. 'Can you smell something burning?'

Grayson let out a swearword and released me to check on the dinner. I let out a breath and tried to get my reeling senses back in order. I watched him move about the kitchen and did all I could to keep my hands off him. It would be so easy to close the distance between us and finish what we had started. But he was only offering a one-night stand and I had no intention of becoming one of his casual lovers.

But I wanted him and that was a problem. A problem I wasn't sure I knew how to handle. I was tempted to sleep with him to do as he said—to get it out of our system. But I had a feeling one night with him would not help in that regard but rather make me want him more. Have you ever tried to eat one piece of popcorn? Not possible, right?

One kiss from Grayson's firm mouth had stirred in me a desire for more.

Much more.

# CHAPTER SIX

GRAYSON PICKED UP the wine bottle that was sitting on the table during our dinner. 'Would you like some more wine?'

I put my hand over the top of my glass. 'No, thanks. I need to keep a clear head.'

His half-smile sent a shiver down my spine, leaving a pool of molten heat at the base. 'Because of what happened before dinner?'

I looked at his mouth and something in my stomach turned over. I could feel heat flooding into my cheeks and my lips began to tingle at the memory of his kiss. 'You know how you said you haven't kissed someone before without it leading to sex? Well, I haven't kissed anyone since my ex.'

He frowned. 'Do you regret breaking it off?'

'No, not at all. We weren't right for each other, but I couldn't see it.' I twisted my mouth and went on, 'I guess I didn't want to see it. There's a point in a relationship where you put so much time and effort in to keeping it on track that getting out of it seems more difficult than continuing it.' I shifted my wineglass and added, 'I think that's what happened with my parents too. My mother stayed with my father far longer than she should have.'

'They weren't happy?'

'Not particularly. They bickered a lot.' I frowned as I thought about my childhood before my father's death. Summoning up memories of my father made a crushing weight of sadness form in my chest. I had so many good memories of him and yet there were some shadowy ones I didn't like recalling. Memories of him shouting at my mother, slamming doors, and disappearing for days on end. 'I loved my dad, but he could be difficult at times.' I pushed a tiny crumb under the rim of my plate and then chanced a glance at Grayson. 'He was a gifted architect and loved his work. It totally consumed him at times. But I wonder if he was as honest with my mother about how things were going financially.'

'I know you were young at the time, but what were you told about the merger?'

I held his clear grey-blue gaze. 'My mother told me your grandfather had pulled out of the merger at the last minute. There was some disagreement about the terms of the deal and consequently my father lost thousands of pounds. After his death, we were left with virtually nothing. My mother blamed your grandfather to the day she died.'

Grayson was silent for a long moment, a muscle pulsing in the lower quadrant of his jaw. 'My grandfather was a hard-nosed businessman, but he wouldn't have ripped off your father.' The implacable edge to his tone made me uneasy. Had I got it wrong? For all these years I had blamed Grayson's grandfather for the destruction of my father. What if there was another side to the story?

'So, what happened to all my father's money?'

There was a long silence. A painful silence as the reality started to dawn on me. Grayson was not going to besmirch my father's memory by telling me the truth—I had to stumble on it myself. Some of those shadowy memories from my childhood surfaced—memories of arguments about money I didn't understand at the time. But I was starting to understand them now. It was a painful collision between the face-saving narrative my mother had spun and the cold, hard truth.

I swallowed a lightbulb in my throat. The same lightbulb that had just flicked on in my head. 'My father didn't have any money, did he?'

Grayson simply sighed as if he was reluctant to add to my pain at finding out my adored father was not the man I had thought him to be.

'For all these years, I've blamed your grandfather...' My voice trailed off as my mind drifted to all the conversations I'd had with my mother after my father's death. She hadn't got on with him while they were married, but in death she had glorified him, making him out to be the perfect husband. But I vaguely remember the arguments about his recklessness with money. Arguments that were conducted behind closed doors, so Niamh and I weren't privy to the details. In a child's mind, a parent can do no wrong, especially when they were a fun parent who was so generous with gifts and words of praise. But now I was seeing my father through an adult's eyes and what I had taken for spontaneity and generosity back then may well be seen as a lack of maturity and responsibility now.

I pushed back my chair and rose from the table, crossing my arms over my body, trying to contain my burgeoning emotions. 'I wish my mother had told me the truth after my father died. Surely, she owed me that?'

Grayson came up behind me and placed his hands on the tops of my shoulders. His touch was warm and grounding, and I was grateful for it as my world was still spinning on its axis.

'I'm sorry you had to find out this way.' His voice was deep and full of compassion, and it made it harder for me to find my dislike of him. But did I dislike him at all now? If his explosive kiss hadn't been enough to flick the switch on my feelings, his care and consideration over the last few minutes was enough to send me into emotional territory I had never been before. Not even with my ex.

I turned in his hold and looked up into his concerned gaze. 'You weren't going to spell out my father's wrongs, were you?'

His mouth twisted in a rueful fashion. His hands remained lightly on top of my shoulders, and I did nothing to move away. 'It's hard when those we love and admire the most let us down.'

'Your father too, huh?'

Grayson gave a grim movement of his lips. 'I was always closer to my grandfather, to be honest. My father wasn't and isn't reliable. He promised and didn't deliver. My grandfather, on the other hand, was honourable and true to his word.'

My gaze drifted to his mouth seemingly of its own volition. 'I'm sorry for thinking such bad thoughts about him all this time.'

Grayson smiled a lopsided smile and gave my shoulders a gentle squeeze. 'You were a kid. You believed what you were told. He wouldn't have held it against you.'

'I wonder why my mother allowed me to believe my father was betrayed so badly by your grandfather. I mean, she didn't have the most loving relationship with him. They fought all the time. But after he died, it was a different story. He was the most amazing husband in the world, blah blah blah.'

'Most mothers like to protect their kids from uncomfortable truths,' Grayson said. 'Grief can stir up a host of emotions, guilt being one of them.'

There was a beat or two of silence. A silence so intense I could hear the rustle of his shirt as he lifted his hand to my face. His fingertip stroked the curve of my cheek, and I shivered in reaction. What was it about his touch that put my senses on high alert?

'You're touching me again.'

'So I am.' His finger travelled down to my mouth, and I let out a soft gasp of pleasure as his finger brushed across the surface of my lips. 'Would you like me to stop?'

'No.' My voice was soft and breathless, and my self-control was missing in action. I moved closer to him at the same time he moved closer to me. Our bodies collided with a combustible impact I felt in every cell in my flesh. Scorching heat flashed through me, lighting spot fires in my blood. Our mouths came together in a desperate kiss, a kiss that spoke of primal yearnings that were no longer under control. His tongue met mine and the bottom dropped out of my stomach. His tongue was insistent, as urgent and passionate as mine. I could not get enough of his taste. I could not get close enough to the hard contours of his body. My blood was boiling with lust and there was nothing I could do about it.

'You have to tell me to stop.' Grayson's voice had a rough edge that sent another shudder ricocheting through my body.

'Maybe I don't want you to stop,' I said in a husky whisper, sweeping my tongue across his lower lip. 'Maybe I want you to make love to me.'

He held me in a tight grip, his fingers almost biting into the flesh of my upper arms. 'You'd agree to a one-night stand?'

I linked my arms around his neck, pressing my lower body to the burgeoning heat and hardness of his. 'Maybe one night won't be enough for you.' I injected my tone with flirty playfulness but inside I was praying he wouldn't settle for one night, that he would want more than a casual encounter. Not a long-term commitment by any means, just a little fling to scratch the itch, so to speak. And what an itch it had become. It was a fever in my blood and, if his hard body pressing against me was any indication, it was raging in his as well.

His eyes blazed with longing and my self-esteem rose a few notches higher than it had ever been before. Had anyone looked at me with such raw naked lust? Had anyone made me feel more desirable? More beautiful and feminine? Not in this lifetime.

'One night. I can't promise more than that.' There was a hint of regret in his tone, and it made me even more determined to get him to change his mind.

I toyed with the ends of his hair at the back of his head, my chest pressed tightly against his. 'Then we'd better make the most of it.' I pressed my mouth to his but within a heartbeat he took control of the kiss. His lips crushed mine beneath his, the passion firing between us like highly flammable fuel. My spine turned to liquid and my insides coiled tight with need. His hands came up to frame my face, his lips still moving against mine with molten heat. His tongue commanded entry and I opened to him, my lower body tingling at the anticipation of welcoming his intimate invasion.

'God, I want you so bad,' he groaned against my mouth, his hands going to my hips, holding me close to his arousal.

'I want you too.' I was barely capable of speech, my breathing was so hectic, my pulse off the scale.

Grayson dragged his mouth off mine and grasped my hands in his, holding me apart from his body. 'Not here. I want you in my bed.'

I had almost forgotten we were still in the dining room with the remains of our dinner still on the table. I waved a hand vaguely in the direction of the table. 'Shouldn't we clear up first?'

'Later.' His mouth came down firmly on mine and I was left in no doubt of his priorities. Clearing up after dinner was clearly nowhere near the top of his list of must-do tasks.

I barely remembered how we got to his bedroom on the next floor. Our journey passed in a blur of kisses and caresses that made the blood sing in my veins. He shouldered open the door of his bedroom and I followed him inside. He allowed me a few moments to glance around at the luxurious furnishings, not to mention the king-sized bed with its snowy white linen and array of pillows.

'Nice bedroom,' I said.

'It does the job.'

I arched a brow. 'For sleeping and sex?'

'Just sleeping.'

I frowned in puzzlement. 'What do you mean?'

He closed the door with a soft click, his eyes dark and lustrous. 'You're the first women I've brought home.'

'You've lived here ten years and never slept with a lover here? Are you flipping serious?'

He began to undo the buttons of his shirt, his eyes still holding mine in a lock that sent a delicate shiver rolling down the backs of my legs. 'I don't like sharing my space with strangers.' He shrugged himself out of his shirt and tossed it over the back of a carved walnut chair.

'So, you only sleep with strangers?'

'Mostly.'

'You know, a psychologist would have plenty to say about that.'

He gave a nonchalant shrug. 'They might have plenty to say about you remaining celibate since you dumped your ex.'

'Yes, well, I've been busy with work and stuff.'

He came over to me and lifted my chin with his finger. 'You can change your mind, you know.'

'About sleeping with you?'

His eyes glinted. 'I'm not sure we'll do much sleeping.'

I drew in a shaky breath, my body unravelling at the potent closeness of him. 'Good to know. I would hate to waste a minute in your bed snoring my head off.'

He grinned and reached for me, tugging me against his body. 'Why don't you get undressed?'

'Why don't you undress me?' Wow, who was this bold and brazenly flirty woman? I had morphed into someone else, someone I didn't recognise as myself. But I liked the sense of power it gave me to be open about what I wanted.

'With pleasure. Turn around.'

I did as he commanded. His hand went to the zip at the back of my dress, and he rolled it down slowly, so slowly I was quaking and shuddering by the time he pulled it to the small of my back. His warm fingers caressed my bare skin before he eased the straps off my shoulders, the dress falling in a black silky puddle at my feet. I was wearing a black strapless push-up bra and matching lace knickers and my high heels.

Grayson turned me to face him, his eyes feasting on my form, and I could not remember a time when I had felt sexier and more feminine or more powerful. 'You are so damn gorgeous.' There was a breathless quality to his voice that delighted me no end. Even though I knew he had seen countless women in nothing but their underwear or even less, I could feel myself glowing from his praise.

I placed my hands on his naked chest, revelling in the texture of his skin and the light dusting of his chest hair. 'Are you going to take your trousers off or will I do it for you?'

His hooded gaze smouldered. 'Feel free.'

My hands went to the waistband of his trousers, my heart thrashing around in my chest. I tried not to fumble but I was so turned on my fingers would barely cooperate. I finally undid the snap button and took the toggle of his zip between my finger and thumb. I gave him an arch look. 'I wonder what I'll find under here?'

'Only one way of finding out.'

I rolled the zip down and gazed in wonder at the considerable tenting of his underwear. My lower body grew damp with longing and my pulse pounded. 'Mmm…impressive.'

His hands came up to cup my breasts and even

though I was still wearing a bra, I could feel the magical heat of his touch through the barrier of lace. 'I want to touch you all over.' His voice was gravel-rough, and it sent a shockwave of ferocious lust through my body.

'I want to touch you too.' I stroked my finger-tip down the length of him through his underwear, and he shuddered and groaned.

His hands went to the clasp of my bra. 'May I?'

'Please do.'

He unclipped my bra and it fell away from my body and dropped to the floor. His eyes drank in my shape and then his hands gently caressed my breasts, sending shivers through my flesh. My nipples were tight buds, and he lowered his mouth to them in turn, the delightful sensations rippling through my body. He stroked his tongue over my breast, a light, barely touching caress, but it sent tongues of flame through my blood.

I whimpered in pleasure as his lips and tongue explored every inch of my breasts, never had they been subjected to such intimate attention.

Finally, he straightened and looked me directly in the eye. 'You still want to do this?'

'I do. You?'

His smile was crooked, and he tugged me against him, pelvis to pelvis. Heat coursed through my body in a scorching wave that made my legs tremble. 'What do you think?'

'I'm not sure I'm capable of thinking right now,' I said, relishing the rock-hard bulge of him against me. 'You've scrambled my brains.'

His mouth came down to just above mine, his warm breath teasing my lips. 'You've done a pretty good job on mine too.' And then his mouth sealed mine in a kiss that set my lips on fire.

But kissing wasn't enough for either of us. Within seconds his mouth was back on my right breast, licking and sucking and pleasuring my naked flesh until I was breathless with need.

Grayson walked me backwards to his bed and somewhere along the way I kicked off my high-heeled shoes. His shoes and socks and trousers and underwear landed on the floor nearby. He laid me on the bed and stood looking down at me. I should have felt exposed and vulnerable under the searing heat of his gaze but instead I felt powerfully female.

'I need to get a condom.' He bent down to retrieve his wallet from the bedside table, deftly removing the protection from its packet and applying it to his swollen length. I could not take my eyes off him if I tried.

He came down beside me on the bed, leaning his weight on one elbow as he stroked his other hand down the length of my body, from my breasts to my thighs and back again. It was a slow, leisurely movement, as if he had all the time in the world, but my body was screaming for him in a silently throbbing ache between my legs that was almost like pain.

Grayson hooked one leg over one of mine, his mouth going back to my breast. I arched my back and gave myself up to the sensation of his lips and tongue on my skin. He moved his mouth down to the underside of my breast, his tongue moving in a slow stroke that made my toes curl and my desire for him skyrocket. He moved his mouth to the sensitive skin just below my ear and I shivered as his lips fluttered against me.

'You probably have no idea how long I've wanted to do this,' he said in a growly voice that sent another wave of molten heat to my core.

'Really?' To say I was a little shocked would be an understatement. I angled my head to look at him. 'You're very good at keeping your cards close. Just about every time I've ever looked at you, you were frowning.'

He pressed a brief kiss to my mouth with just enough pressure to make my pulse race. 'I'm not frowning now.'

I ran a fingertip around the gentle curve of his mouth. 'You don't look half as threatening when you smile. You should do it more often.'

He brushed his thumb across my lower lip, his gaze holding mine. 'So should you.'

I twisted my lips in a self-deprecating manner.

'I had crooked teeth when I was a kid. I guess I forgot how to smile, even when I got them straightened.' I waited a beat and then added, 'But then I didn't have too much to smile about after my dad's death and then Niamh's accident.'

Grayson stroked a wayward strand of hair away from my face, his expression thoughtful. 'I'm sorry life dealt you such a rough hand, but you mustn't blame yourself for either event. You were a kid. Sometimes bad stuff just happens.'

I didn't want to talk about my childhood and was annoyed at myself and embarrassed for bringing it up during such an intimate moment. I placed one of my hands on the side of his face, his light stubble tickling the flesh of my palm. I adopted a playful tone and asked, 'Do you have such deep and meaningful conversations with all your casual lovers?'

A flicker of something crossed his features like a sudden waft off air across a still body of water. 'Not usually.'

'What do you talk about?'

'Not much.'

'The weather?'

'Occasionally.' His gaze went to my mouth and my lips tingled in anticipation.

I brought my hand back down to his chest, laying in flat against his right pectoral muscle.

His skin was like hot satin under my hand, and I longed to explore every inch of his body.

'Are you nervous?' His question caught me by surprise, mostly because I didn't think I had shown any sign of nervousness. But sleeping with a new partner was always a little tricky for me. What if I didn't turn them on? What if I made too much noise or not enough? And then there were all the body issues I had tried so hard to dispense with over the years. Somehow Grayson had picked up on my feelings and that was almost as threatening, *more* threatening, than him seeing me naked. I usually avoided emotional vulnerability at all costs. But being with him made me want to expose more of myself, my true self. My secret self.

I chewed at my lower lip, averting my gaze from his probing one. 'It's been a while since I…was with anyone…'

Grayson lifted my chin, so my gaze met his once more. 'Because you're not over your ex?'

I scrunched up my face at the ridiculous notion of me nursing a broken heart over Ryan. How could I ever have thought we had what it took to have a good relationship?

'I was over him the moment he made it clear Niamh wasn't welcome in our lives going forward.' I sighed and went on, 'I should've seen it a lot earlier, of course, but I ignored the red flags.'

Grayson brushed another strand of hair away

from my face. 'A lot of people don't understand how much we love and feel responsible for our less able-bodied siblings. It's more than blood being thicker than water. I don't think a day goes past without me worrying about Ethan's future.'

'Nor me with Niamh.'

He held my gaze for a long beat.

'We can't let them rush into anything they can't undo,' he said. 'A fling is fine; marriage is another thing entirely.'

'Yes, it is, but if we're too against them marrying it could backfire and make them all the more determined.'

His gaze went to my mouth. 'Like what happened with us?' He gave a slow rueful smile and continued, 'I told myself I wasn't going to touch you and look at us now. There's barely a part of our bodies that isn't touching.'

'You're not touching my mouth.'

'I can soon fix that.' He lowered his lips to mine, and I lost myself in the potent heat and fire of his kiss. After a few breathless moments, he broke the kiss to look at me through sexily hooded eyes. 'Anywhere else I've neglected to touch?'

I shivered at the rough edge to his voice and the determined glint in his gaze. 'I think you missed the side of my left breast.'

'I'll see to it right now.' He kissed his way down the side of my neck, covering every inch of my skin with soft fluttering movements of his lips that set my nerves dancing. By the time he came to my left breast, I was whimpering. His touch was so light and yet so electric, stirring my desire for him to fever-pitch.

'And I don't think I touched you here,' he said, moving his mouth down to my belly button.

I sucked in my breath and shuddered as his tongue circled the tiny whorl of my navel. He moved further down to the seam of my body, and I forgot to breathe when his lips and tongue explored my female flesh. Oh, and I forgot to think as well. Sensations I had never experienced before rippled through my body in crashing waves. I panted, I gasped, I cried, and I arched my back in ecstasy as the shockwaves coursed through me.

'Well, that's never happened before,' I said on an expelled breath of wonder.

Grayson shifted position so I was eye to eye with him. He stroked a lazy hand down the flank of my still quivering thigh. 'What do you mean?'

'I've never been able to come like that.' I lowered my gaze a fraction and confessed, 'I always used to pretend.'

He lifted my chin, so my gaze locked on his again. There was no judgement or criticism in his expression but rather a look of gentle compassion that totally ambushed my feelings. I was trying *so* hard not to be infatuated with him, to keep my feelings out of our one-night stand. But it was almost impossible not to open my heart a teensy-weensy crack.

'I'm glad you feel comfortable with me.' He stroked a slow-moving finger across my lower lip, sending tingles to my toes and back.

I threaded my fingers through his hair, my lower body aching for him all over again. 'I've thought of another place you haven't touched me.'

His smouldering gaze sent another wave of searing heat through my core. 'Really? How remiss of me. I must be losing my touch.'

Grayson Barlowe definitely wasn't losing his touch as far as I was concerned, but I was in danger of losing my mind, or worse—my heart. What came next was the most dazzling encounter of my life. He held me as I shuddered through another spectacular orgasm, and I held him as he shuddered through his own powerful release. We lay in each other's arms for a long time afterwards, neither of us speaking, our ragged breathing gradually returning to normal the only sound in the silence.

Finally, I found the courage to turn my head and look at him lying beside me. He had his eyes closed but as if he sensed my gaze resting on him, he turned his head and met my gaze.

'Hey,' he said in a gravel-rough tone, the fingers of his left hand entwining with the fingers of my right hand. He gave my fingers a gentle squeeze. 'You okay?'

'Why wouldn't I be okay? I've just had multiple orgasms for the first time ever.' I injected a playful note to my tone but inside I was still reeling from the passion that had transpired between us. The sort of passion I had never experienced before. Passion that left my body singing and tingling and fizzing in the afterglow.

Grayson rolled onto his side and leaned his weight on one elbow, his gaze still trained on mine. 'You're a very responsive lover.' He slowly circled one of my nipples with his finger and I trembled anew.

'Who knew two enemies could get it on with such success?' I was still determined to keep my playful persona in place, but it felt odd, like wearing a jumper back to front and inside out.

His finger traced a circle around my other nipple, and I bit back a tiny gasp of pleasure. 'Is that how you see us? As enemies?' he asked.

I gave a little shrug and shifted my gaze from the probing heat of his. 'We're not exactly friends, are we?'

There was a long beat of silence.

'We might have to be if Ethan and Niamh stay together,' Grayson said. 'Will that be a problem for you? I mean, after tonight?'

I worked hard to school my features into impassivity. 'No. That was the deal, right? One night only.'

His gaze drifted to my mouth and my pulse began to pound. 'I should take you home.'

I had no idea of the time, but I knew it was way past my bedtime. 'You should.'

'But I'm not going to.'

'Oh, really?'

His eyes glinted with unbridled lust that re-ignited my own. 'I'm not finished with you yet.' And before I could think of a response, his mouth came down on mine.

## CHAPTER SEVEN

I WOKE TO the sound of the morning chorus of birds in the trees outside Grayson's bedroom window and the hum of traffic and it took me a moment to reorient myself. The bed was empty beside me, but I could see the imprint of Grayson's head on the pillow next to mine. My stomach hollowed out at the memory of all we had done together during the night. I stretched my legs out against the silky sheets and breathed in the scent of him like I was breathing in a potent drug I couldn't resist.

But I *had* to resist.

We had made an agreement and I was not going to be the one who begged for him to change it.

I threw off the sheet covering me and began to search for my clothes. They weren't on the floor where I had last seen them but were now neatly folded on the walnut chair. I snatched them up and put them on with as much haste as I could muster, given I'd only had a couple of hours sleep, if that. There wasn't time for a shower, although I would have loved one. I had to put my game face on and get the hell out of Grayson's house before I was tempted to pop a toothbrush in his bathroom.

I opened the bedroom door to leave just as he came in carrying a tray with a mug of coffee and some toast on it. I was in such a rush, I collided with the tray and the mug toppled over, splashing coffee all over the front of my dress. Lucky it was black—the dress, not the coffee, although that too was black—but the coffee was steaming hot, and I yelped and pulled my dress away from my stomach.

'Are you okay?' Grayson asked, putting the tray to one side.

'You could have knocked before you came in,' I said, throwing him a glare so icy it should have frozen him on the spot.

'Last time I checked, it was my bedroom.' His tone was as snippy as mine but then he let out a long uneven breath. 'Sorry. That was uncalled for. Blame it on the lack of sleep.'

'Well, that's your fault too.' I wasn't angry about the coffee. I was angry I was so touched that he'd brought it to me. It didn't seem to fit with the one-night stand arrangement we had made. No one had ever brought me coffee and toast in the morning, not my ex, not even Niamh, mostly because I was always up first.

'Did I burn you?' The concern in Grayson's voice and in his expression dissolved my anger on the spot and opened the teensy-weensy crack in my heart a little further.

I released a sigh. 'No, I overreacted. I'm sorry. You just surprised me, is all.'

He placed a gentle hand on the top of one of my shoulders, his eyes holding mine in such a tender lock my breath caught in my throat.

'You surprised me too.' His voice was deep and husky, and I wasn't completely sure he was talking about the coffee incident or not. Something about the glint in his grey-blue eyes made me wonder if he was recalling every passionate moment we had shared in his bed.

I could feel a blush flowing into my cheeks. Some of those moments in his bed were pretty damn hot. It would probably take me months to forget about them. Years, decades, a lifetime.

'I'm going to be late for work if I don't get a wriggle on. Thank you for…dinner and…erm…' I couldn't finish the sentence and instead forced my lips into a vestige of a smile.

Grayson brought me a little closer, the warm, clean, fresh scent of him making my senses do cartwheels. How could he look so good after so little sleep? 'Are you free tomorrow night?'

I blinked like an owl. 'Why?'

'We should at least put some ideas on the table for Ethan and Niamh's house.'

I had forgotten all about my sister and Ethan's dream house to go with their dream relationship. But would working with Grayson be a dream or a nightmare? Especially now we had done the once-only deed.

'Oh, right, yes, I guess so.'

His hand fell away from my shoulder, but he was still standing within touching distance.

'I figure if we show we're willing to work at it together, it might make them less defensive and more introspective about their plans to marry.'

'Building a house together is a big commitment. Does Ethan have the money to do it? Niamh has some savings but nowhere near enough to—'

'He has plenty of money. I oversee the bulk of it, but he has the freedom to spend his allowance and the income he gets from working for me as he sees fit. It helps him feel more independent.'

'So, he has a real job in your company? Not just a token position?'

A frown pulled at his brow. 'But of course. He'd have been insulted if I had given him anything less than a real position. He uses some quite complicated computer software with our design team. It takes him a little longer than he'd like but we make allowances for that.'

'He's so lucky to have you in his corner.'

A fleeting shadow passed through his gaze. 'We're lucky to have him. It could've been so different.'

'Yes…' I chewed at my lower lip and lowered my gaze, thinking of how different my sister's life would have been if I hadn't been distracted at the playground. How could one tiny mistake have such irreparable consequences?

Grayson's hand came back down on my shoulder. 'Hey.'

I raised my gaze to mesh with his. I could so easily drown in those eyes. I could so easily lose myself in a fantasy of being with him longer than one night. I could so easily fancy myself falling in love with him. I slammed the brakes on the thought and gave him a stiff smile and turned for the door. 'I must go. I have a client waiting.'

'I'll drive you.'

'No, it'll be quicker on the Tube, but thanks anyway.'

'Ash.' The sound of my name on his lips was almost my undoing. Almost. His voice reverberated in my body, sending my blood racing. But I had to be strong. I had to steel my resolve to keep my emotions out of our 'working' relationship.

I turned to look at him, schooling my features into an impassivity I was nowhere near feeling. 'Yes?'

His eyes were unwavering as they held mine.

'It's probably best if we don't mention what happened between us last night to Ethan and Niamh.'

'Of course.' I made a zipping motion with my hand across my mouth and added, 'No kissing and telling from me.'

One corner of his mouth lifted in a half-smile. 'Where would you like to meet to discuss the project? My office or yours or somewhere neutral?'

'Your office will be fine.'

There was an infinitesimal moment of silence.

'Checking out the enemy territory?' There was a teasing note in his voice and a glint in his eye.

'You betcha,' I said and, giving him a finger wave, turned on my heel and left.

I got home that night after work to find Niamh there. A couple of days ago that would have been entirely normal, but since she had announced her engagement to Ethan she hadn't been home at all.

'Where's Ethan?' I asked, putting my briefcase down. 'I thought you two were inseparable.'

'He has a late gym session today. I thought it would be a good chance for us to hang out and discuss the wedding. I have some ideas for my dress. Do you want to see?' She scrolled through her phone and then turned the screen so I could see it. 'What do you think?'

It was exactly the sort of dress my sister

adored—snow-white with lots of tulle, and a classical bridal veil and a train that was metres long.

'Mmm, lovely.'

Niamh tilted her head and studied me for a moment. 'Are you okay?'

'I'm fine.' I ran a hand through my hair and let out a sigh. 'It's been a long day.'

Niamh sat beside me. 'Where were you last night?'

'I was…out.' I didn't want to blatantly lie to my sister, nor did I want to tell her where I had been. I could barely think of where I had been and who I was with and what we had done without a whole-body blush.

'Out *all* night?'

I blinked. 'How did you know I was out?'

She lifted her phone and clicked on the app that tracked her whereabouts and mine. Funny, but I had forgotten she could check where I was at any time of the day. 'You were at Grayson's house last night.'

How could I deny it? She had seen the evidence on her phone. 'Yes, well, we had things to discuss, so—'

'Like what?'

I rose from the sofa and smoothed my hands down my dress. 'You and Ethan for one.'

Niamh's eyes took on a stubborn light. 'You

don't think I'm ready for marriage but I am. I love Ethan and he loves me.'

'I'm happy for you, I really am. It's just I agree with Grayson that you're rushing it a bit.'

'Is it because of his disability or mine?'

'No, of course not. But both must be factored in when you plan your life together. Relationships are hard at the best of times, but you and Ethan have other obstacles most people don't have to face. You have to be realistic about what to expect. You'll need support.'

'But we'll have each other.'

'It might not be enough.'

Niamh picked at her fingers—a nervous habit she had developed since the accident. 'But you'll be around, won't you?' She was looking at her fingers rather than meeting my gaze.

I bent down in front of her where she was sitting on the sofa, and I put my hands on both of her knees. 'I will always be around to support you.'

Her gaze met mine briefly and then shifted back to stare at her hands. 'But what if you fall in love and get married one day?'

'I am *not* going to fall in love and get married.' I may have sounded a little too adamant about the falling in love bit because… Grayson. I couldn't get him out of my mind. I could still feel the press of his lips, the stroke and glide of his hands, the powerful, passionate possession of his male body in mine.

Niamh's gaze met mine. 'Why don't you want to fall in love again? It's the best feeling in the world.'

I took one of her hands and held it in mine. 'I wasn't in love with Ryan, I just thought I was at the time. That's why it's so important not to rush things.' Who am I to talk after sleeping with Grayson Barlowe last night? If that wasn't rushing things, I don't know what was, but I couldn't help myself.

'You were with Ryan for three years,' Niamh pointed out. 'How could you not have known you weren't in love with him?'

I released her hand and straightened with a sigh. 'On one level, I think I probably did realise it wasn't the real deal, but it took a lot longer than it should have for me to admit it.' I painted a smile on my lips and added, 'Now, enough about the past. Are you staying for dinner?'

Niamh got off the sofa. 'No, I'm meeting Ethan back at the gym, his session will be over soon. I just wanted to pick up a couple of things and check on you.'

I frowned in confusion. I was the one who checked on her, not her on me. 'Why would you feel the need to check on me?'

She gave me an unreadable look that was slightly unnerving, to say the least. 'You spent the night with Grayson Barlowe.' Her tone didn't contain any hint of disapproval or accusation but rather was stating an indisputable fact.

I licked my suddenly dry lips. 'We had dinner and talked about stuff.'

'You must've had a lot to talk about. Every time I checked my phone, you were still there.'

I could feel heat storming into my cheeks and other parts of my body. But I comforted myself that Niamh couldn't have possibly checked her phone all through the night. She had to sleep after all.

'It was a late night,' I said. 'But I managed to avoid getting into an argument with him.'

Niamh tilted her head and narrowed her gaze like an inquisitive bird. 'So, you're starting to like him?'

I pursed my lips for a moment, wondering why my sister was so interested in my feelings about her fiancé's older brother. I expelled a short breath and decided to lure her away from the conversation. 'Do you need a lift to the gym?'

'No, Ethan booked a car for me. It should be here any minute.' She glanced at the rideshare app on her phone and added, 'It's just pulling up outside now.' She came over and gave me a hug and a kiss. 'Can you and Grayson come to dinner on Saturday night? Ethan and I would like to cook for you both.'

My sister wasn't exactly a gourmet cook, but

then I had done most of the cooking for her. I only hoped Ethan had a few more skills in the kitchen than her. I suspected they were determined to show they could look after themselves, to convince Grayson and me that they were ready for marriage.

'That sounds…nice.'

'Great. I'll see you then.' Niamh grabbed her tote bag in one hand and another small bag of clothes in the other. 'See you on Saturday. Shall we say eight p.m.?'

'Eight it is.'

I turned up at Grayson's office the following evening, but his secretary informed me he was still with a client.

'He's running over time, but he shouldn't be too much longer. Would you like a drink while you wait?' she asked.

'I'm fine, thank you.' I sat in the waiting area on a butter-soft leather sofa and picked up one of the glossy magazines, leafing through the pages without much concentration. I was trying to be cool and calm about seeing Grayson in a work capacity, but it was hard to get the memory of his intimate touch out of my head. I put the magazine down and glanced around my surroundings instead. Fresh flowers were on the glass and marble coffee table next to the stack of magazines. Plush cream carpet covered the floor, and the furniture was modern and stylish and luxuriously comfortable. In fact, so comfortable, I had sunk so far down into the caramel-coloured leather sofa I was wondering how I was going to get out of it.

Soft carpet notwithstanding, I heard Grayson's slightly uneven footsteps coming towards me. I looked up and gave him a formal smile. 'How's your day been?'

'Busy. Yours?'

'So-so.' I tried to rise from the sofa without success.

'Here, let me help you.' He offered me his hand and, with only a moment's hesitation, I placed my hand in his warm strong one. A shiver cascaded down my spine and a flashpoint of heat shot to my core. His fingers were firm around mine—they had to be in order to get me out of the sofa—as he pulled me to my feet. I was standing almost toe to toe with him, and I forgot how to breathe. His aftershave teased my nostrils and I ached to lean closer to feel his arms go around me as they had the other night.

'Thank you,' I said. 'Erm…you can let go of my hand now. I promise I won't fall over.' I'm not sure I could promise that—my legs weren't feeling too steady. Just being in his presence was enough to undo me, ligament by ligament.

'Oh, sorry.' He pulled his hand away as if he had

forgotten he had been holding it. 'Come this way.' On the way past his secretary's desk, he said, 'You can go now, Caroline. Thanks for staying back.'

'No problem,' Caroline said with a smile that encompassed me as well.

I walked with Grayson down the wide corridor to his office. He pushed open the door and indicated for me to go in first and I stepped past him and swept my gaze over the layout. Floor to ceiling windows overlooking the River Thames took up one side of his office, and on another side was floor to ceiling bookshelves. A couple of pieces of artwork hung on one wall and his qualifications hung on the other, but somehow I suspected they were there to reassure his clients that he had the necessary qualifications, rather than from any personal pride in his achievements. I scanned every surface but couldn't see any of the architectural awards he had won.

'Would you like a drink before we get started?'

'Erm, what were you thinking of having?' I asked.

His eyes drifted to my mouth and my stomach somersaulted. 'If I told you that, we might not get any work done.' There was a gleam in his grey-blue gaze that sent another shiver rolling down my spine.

I moistened my suddenly dry lips, my heart picking up its pace. 'I thought we weren't going to mention what happened the other night.' My voice came out a little husky and breathless.

Grayson came to stand right in front of me. He was so close I could smell the sharp citrus notes of his aftershave and the clean laundered fragrance of his shirt. He picked up a loose strand of my hair and tucked it gently behind my ear and my legs almost folded beneath me at his touch. 'We can tweak the rules a bit.'

'We can?'

'If you want to.'

'Do you want to?' My voice was still too breathless, too husky, too desperate.

His eyes moved back and forth between each of mine before dipping once more to my mouth. 'I want to.' His hands came down to settle on my hips and he tugged me closer until I was against the firm wall of his body. 'God, how I want to.' And then his mouth covered mine.

It was a kiss that sent rivers of fire through my blood and flames of need through my body. His tongue flirted with mine in an erotic dance that stirred my senses into overdrive. I was addicted to the taste of him, the hint of mint and good quality coffee that was my new passion.

He groaned as he deepened the kiss, and I made some breathless sounds as his tongue mated with mine. He finally lifted his mouth away, his hands still holding me by the hips. 'I told myself this wasn't going to happen.' His voice was deep and rusty, his breathing almost as ragged as mine. 'I told myself it mustn't happen.'

'We're both consenting adults, right?'

His eyes held mine in an intimate lock. 'I don't do relationships. This can only be a fling.'

'I don't do relationships either.'

He studied me for a beat. 'I couldn't get you out of my mind.'

'Nice to know I left a lasting impression.'

He gave a crooked smile and tugged me even closer. I could feel the delicious ridge of his erection and my body secretly prepared itself. 'I want you.'

'I want you too.' I moved against him and added with a sultry smile, 'I'm just better at hiding it.'

He growled against my mouth, and I opened to him again. His kiss was even more passionate, and I was with him all the way. One of his hands slid up my ribcage to settle just below my breast. It was the most exquisite torture to have his hand so close to my tingling flesh. But I liked that about him, that he didn't rush things. He took his time unravelling me, as if it gave him pleasure to pleasure me. Somehow, we managed to get our clothes off, and I was shocked again at how comfortable I was with him seeing me naked. I couldn't hide anything from him, and nor did I want to.

'You are so damn gorgeous,' he said, roving his gaze over my body.

'You look pretty good yourself.' I pressed my lips to the base of his neck and began to work my way down his chest.

His hand came to rest in the small of my back and I relished the delicious sensation of his long fingers splayed against my lower spine. 'Come back up here. I want to kiss you again.'

We kissed some more but I was becoming impatient. I took him in my hands and stroked his steely length. He groaned and moved against me in pleasure and my inner core grew hot and damp with desire. He tore his mouth away from mine and muttered something about getting a condom. Within moments he was back, condom in place, and I was laid back on his desk and he was between my open thighs. Not to possess me but to subject me to the most glorious attention from his lips and tongue. I closed my eyes and gave myself up to the rapture of it. It was intimate and erotic in a way I had never experienced before. I swear I rattled the pens on his desk when I came. It was an earth-shattering orgasm that swept through my body like a tidal wave. It left no part of me unaffected. My toes curled, my fingertips tingled, my back arched, and my heart threatened to pump its way out of my chest.

I lay gasping on my back on his desk, unable

to move, unable to think clearly, unable to find my voice.

Grayson stroked a lazy hand along my thigh, and I shuddered under his caress. 'You looked like you had a good time.'

I leaned up on my elbows to look at him. 'Who knew desk sex could be so much fun?'

'You haven't had desk sex before?'

'No, my experiences in the adventurous sex department are, sadly, quite limited.'

A glint shone in his eyes, and I shuddered again. 'I'll have to do something about that.' There was an erotic promise in his voice that set my pulse racing.

I scrambled to my feet in front of his desk, and he gathered me close, his mouth meeting mine once more in a spine-tingling kiss that left me in no doubt of how aroused he was. It stoked my own desire again and I was soon whimpering for more than a kiss.

Within a few moments we were lying on the floor in a tangle of limbs. Grayson entered me with a deep guttural groan of pleasure, and I relished the feel of his potent length. He set a slow pace at first, each thrust careful and measured, but I wanted him to lose control, to give in to the powerful urges that he was holding in check. I writhed beneath him, whispering my need for him to go faster, harder, and he increased his pace, carrying me with him on a rollercoaster ride of primal lust. I was aware of every part of his body where it was in contact with mine—his lips on my lips, his chest pressed against my breasts, his hipbones against mine, his intimate possession that stretched me, filled me, thrilled me. The sensations rolled through me, picking me up and tossing me about like a piece of flotsam on a raging sea. I cried out loud at the sheer force of it rippling and then rocking through my flesh. I lifted my hips on his downward thrusts, the connection as electrifying as two powerful currents meeting. Grayson suddenly thrust deeper, pitching forward as his own release powered through him. I held him as he shook and shuddered in my arms, wondering why I had allowed myself to be so short-changed with sex in the past. This was how it was meant to be—a mutual giving and taking of pleasure.

Grayson lay across me, his head buried against the side of my neck. 'Am I too heavy for you?'

'No.' I stroked one of my hands down the length of his spine and he shivered under my touch. I decided I liked the weight of him pinning me to the floor. I liked his legs entangled with mine. I liked everything about making love with him. I liked *everything* about him, which was a problem because I wasn't supposed to allow my feelings free rein during our fling.

After a long moment he propped himself up on

his hands to look down at me. 'How about office floor sex? Have you had that before?'

'Nope.'

His sexily hooded eyes went to my mouth. 'I hope I didn't give you carpet burn.'

I linked my hands around his neck and gazed into his eyes. 'If you did, it was worth it.'

His smile made something fall from a height in my belly. 'Roll over and I'll check.'

I turned over and lay my head on my crossed over arms on the floor. Grayson stroked his hands down the length of my back and over my bottom. His touch set every nerve under my skin dancing, and a new flicker of desire ignited between my thighs.

'No, you're all good.'

'Does this massage come with a happy ending?' I adopted a playful tone.

'Do you want one?'

'At the risk of sounding greedy, yes, I do.'

He stroked his hand down from my neck to the curve of my buttocks and I shivered in delight. 'I need to get a new condom first.' He moved away to get one and I lay there tingling in anticipation.

I angled my head to look at him. 'Why are you taking so long?'

He stood looking down at me with lust shining in his eyes. 'I'm enjoying the view.'

Until that point, I hadn't noticed the scar that

ran from the top of his thigh to the middle of his left calf muscle. It had faded to white, but it stood out from his tan like a zigzag of lightning.

I rolled over and sat up with my knees bent in front of me. 'Does it still hurt? Your leg, I mean.'

A shadow passed over his face like clouds across the moon. 'Not much.'

'It certainly doesn't hinder your performance in bed or on the desk or on the floor,' I said.

'Good to know.'

A small silence passed.

I rested my chin on my bent knees and bit down on my lower lip. 'Have I killed the mood?'

'What do you think?'

I ran my gaze over his gloriously aroused body and my pulse began to pound. 'I'm thinking no.'

His lips twitched with an almost smile, his eyes dark and gleaming. 'Come here.'

I came. In more ways than one… Just saying…

# CHAPTER EIGHT

IN SPITE OF the earth-shattering lovemaking, we did try to get some ideas on the computer screen for Ethan and Niamh's house, but I sensed Grayson's heart wasn't in it. He didn't want their marriage to go ahead, so why would he want to design a house for them?

I pushed away the computer mouse and sat back on the chair he had placed in front of his desk next to his. 'This isn't really working, is it?' I asked.

He scraped his hand through his hair and sighed. 'It's so soon to be planning a house. They didn't know each other six weeks ago.'

'I've said it before—people can have instant connections.'

He turned his head to look at me and my heart fluttered. 'Do you think your sister really is in love with my brother?'

It was a hard question to answer. 'I think she believes she is.'

He pressed his lips together and looked back at the computer screen. 'They haven't given us a detailed enough brief. Normally, I spend a couple of hours or more with a client on a first consult. We iron out any inconsistencies or council or engineering limitations. It saves them time and money to get it right first time.' He waved his hand at the printed sheet on the desk in disgust. 'This looks like Ethan left it to Niamh to decide what goes where. He should know better; he's worked with me long enough.'

'Sometimes men in love do things they would never normally do. I think it's kind of cute, actually.'

Grayson turned his head to look at me again, his forehead creased in his signature frown. 'There's nothing cute about a house that is impractical for people with the kind of disability my brother has.'

'Maybe Niamh doesn't see Ethan's disability. She just sees the man she loves.'

'Or believes she loves.' His tone was rich with cynicism. 'I wonder if she would love him if he didn't have my grandfather's trust fund.'

I pushed my chair back and stood. 'I think it's time we called it a night.'

Grayson turned his chair to face me, his expression shuttered. 'You're angry.'

I blew out a breath of frustration. 'Of course I'm flipping angry. You keep accusing my sister of being a gold-digger. It's so insulting. I know her well enough to know money and status are not things that impress her. She loves Ethan because of who he is as a person and how he makes her feel.'

'But you said, only minutes ago, you thought she only *believes* she loves him.'

My shoulders went down on a sigh. 'Who can say how anyone really feels? The signs are all there but…' I left my sentence hanging.

'What signs?'

'People in love want to spend lots of time together. They look into each other's eyes a lot; they touch and mirror each other's movements.'

'It's hardly an exact science.'

'No, but it's not without some merit.'

There was a beat or two of silence.

Grayson pushed back his own chair and came to stand in front of me. His hands reached for mine and he gave them a gentle squeeze. 'Still angry with me?'

I gave him an upwards glance from beneath my lowered lashes. 'You haven't apologised yet.'

'I'm sorry.'

'Apology accepted.'

He tipped up my chin with his finger and meshed his gaze with mine. 'Do you want to grab a late dinner somewhere before I take you home?'

My stomach chose that moment to audibly

growl, which made it almost impossible to say I wasn't hungry. 'That would be nice.'

He bent his head to plant a soft kiss on my up-turned mouth. Then he raised his head to lock gazes with me again. 'We're going to have to be careful when we have dinner with Ethan and Niamh on Saturday night. We'll have to make sure we don't show any signs of being involved.'

'Yes, I know, but Niamh already knows I was at your house the other night. She tracked me via the app on her phone. I completely forgot she could do that. I usually keep track of her, not her me.'

Grayson frowned. 'Do you think she suspects anything?'

'I don't think so. I played it pretty cool. I told her we had dinner and talked about stuff. But I do think she's keen for us to like each other because she hates conflict of any sort. It would distress her to think her relationship with Ethan was causing trouble between you and him.'

He placed his hands on my hips and brought me closer. 'It's going to be hard to keep my hands off you.'

I linked my arms around his waist, delighting in the hard contours of his body probing me so in-timately. 'We can make up for it later when we're alone.'

He gave me a wolfish grin that sent a bolt of heat to my core. 'Good plan.'

* * *

We arranged to arrive at Ethan's penthouse separately to avoid any hint of anything going on between us. I arrived a little earlier to see if there was anything I could do to help Niamh, but she was determined to keep me out of the kitchen.

'No, Ethan and I have got this,' she said as she greeted me at the door. 'You go through to the sitting room with a drink and wait for Grayson. Oh, here he is now.'

I turned and looked at Grayson and mumbled an impersonal 'Hi' and he grunted something unintelligible in return.

Niamh shifted her gaze back and forth between us, her forehead creasing in a reproving frown. 'Have you two been bickering again?'

I hastily smothered a laugh by pretending to cough, and Grayson answered before I could think of something to say. I could hardly tell her Grayson and I had been making love, not war, could I?

'We've established a temporary truce, haven't we, Ash?' There was a gleam in his gaze that thankfully Niamh couldn't see for he had turned to face me.

'Indeed, we have,' I said, keeping my expression neutral. Our temporary truce was the code name for our temporary fling. Nothing could be anything but temporary between us, even if Ethan and Niamh did marry.

'That's good because I don't want anything to spoil tonight,' Niamh said. 'Ethan and I have gone to a lot of trouble over dinner.'

Ethan came towards us in his motorised chair with a smile on his face. 'Y-you're t-too generous, babe,' he said, looking meltingly at Niamh. 'You've d-done most of the work.'

It was heart-warming to see the pride Ethan had in my sister. It made Niamh glow like I had never seen her glow before. It also made me feel a little envious. Apart from my sister, I hadn't had anyone in my life who was proud of my achievements. Even before my father died, I can't remember either of my parents being all that impressed by my academic success. And certainly, after Niamh's accident, there was no way my mother would ever draw attention to my stellar school record when my sister's abilities were so damaged. I was glad Niamh now had someone to be proud of her, to support her in any endeavour she made.

Grayson and I ended up in the sitting room with drinks in hand while Ethan and Niamh went back to the kitchen. I took a sip of my champagne and looked at the view over Finsbury Park. How was I going to make small talk with the man who had seen me in my smalls? Who had seen every inch of me? And made love to me for hours?

'You look stunning in that dress,' Grayson said from just behind me.

I turned around and breathed in the citrus scent of him, my heart tripping and skipping and flipping as his gaze ran over me hungrily. 'You're going to give the game away if you keep looking at me like that,' I said in a hushed tone, glancing nervously towards the sitting room door in case my sister or Ethan returned.

'How am I looking at you?'

'Like you want to peel this dress off me and ravish me.'

Grayson's lips curved in a smile, and he lifted his hand to my face and trailed a lazy finger down the slope of my cheek. 'That's exactly what I'd like to do.' His voice was so deep and low it sounded like it was coming from the core of the earth. Speaking of cores—my feminine core was pulsating with liquid heat at being so physically close to him.

My pulse was pounding, my heart hammering, my self-control wavering. I could feel myself swaying towards him as if my body was an iron filing and he was a powerful magnet. 'You'd better hold that thought until later.'

He stepped an inch or two closer and bent his head to brush my lips with a light kiss. Our lips met for the briefest moment, but it was like a match had been struck against bone-dry tinder. Heat, fire, flames, lust burned between our mouths in an explosive combustion. We both made desperate sounds in our throats and our lips and tongues met again. And again.

Grayson finally lifted his mouth off mine, his breathing laboured. 'I don't think I've ever wanted anyone the way I want you.' The gravel-rough sound of his voice sent a shiver down my spine, so too the dark gleam of lust in his gaze.

I reached up with my hand to wipe some of my lip-gloss off his mouth. 'Same.' It was one hundred percent true. I had never felt anything like the level of desire that he stoked in me. Was it because we both knew it was a temporary fling? That it couldn't last, so we had to make the most of it? Was that what was driving us so wild for each other? The clock was ticking and, because of that, every moment we spent together was consumed with our desire to make the most of what we had while we could.

The sound of Ethan's chair approaching the sitting room made me spring back from Grayson as if I had been burnt. But then I had been—burned, singed, fried by a lust so consuming it was making me wander into dangerous territory. The territory of feelings and emotions that had no place in a fling such as ours.

Niamh came in with Ethan and she narrowed her gaze at me. 'What happened to your chin?'

I lifted my fingers to my face, confused by her concern. 'Nothing.'

'It's red like a rash or something,' Niamh said, coming closer to inspect my face.

My stomach dropped as I realised what had caused it—stubble rash. Those stolen kisses had left a red circle of evidence on my chin. 'It's the preservatives in the champagne.' I put my glass down. 'It'll fade in a while.'

'But you've never had a reaction before,' Niamh said.

No, and I had not been kissed so thoroughly before either. 'I've got some cream in my purse. I won't be a minute.' I left the room to go to the bathroom. I closed the door and walked over to the mirror over the basin and grimaced at my reflection. My make-up had been rubbed off, leaving a patch of red where Grayson's stubbly skin had grazed mine. I touched my fingers to the reddish patch and something hot and liquid trickled in my core.

It was like Grayson Barlowe had branded me as his.

I opened my purse and took out a sample tube of my foundation and applied a new layer to disguise the stubble rash. I reapplied some lip-gloss and popped the tube back in my purse, snapping it closed with a click. But there was no cover-up for the shining light in my eyes or the molten heat in my body.

By the time I came out of the bathroom, dinner

was ready in the dining room. Niamh had even gone to the trouble of writing place cards, and I found that I was seated opposite Grayson. His eyes met mine across the table and I had to work hard not to show how much it affected me. But then I felt the gentle brush of his foot against mine and another wave of searing heat flowed to my core.

I found myself eating almost mechanically, saying all the right things in all the right places, such as what a lovely job Niamh had done and how delicious everything was. But, to be honest, I could barely taste a thing. I could only think about how much I wanted Grayson's mouth back on mine.

'Yes, indeed, it's wonderful,' Grayson said, putting down his cutlery. 'Did Ash teach you to cook?'

'Oh, no,' Niamh said with a little self-deprecating laugh. 'She always said I was too messy, or I would burn myself or something.'

'Well, I love your cooking and I think you're amazing at it,' Ethan said, reaching for her hand across the table, his expression warm and tender.

I was temporarily lost for words. Unusual for me, but still, it was a shock to see myself as others saw me—as an over-controlling big sister who was more concerned about keeping the kitchen tidy than whether her disabled sister learned to cook. Had I unconsciously held Niamh back out of guilt? Had I done too much for her to compensate for how I had let her down in that playground by not properly watching her? Had she missed out on learning important life skills out of my guilt?

And, even more important, was I *still* underestimating her capability?

'I'll go and get dessert,' Niamh said, rising from the table. 'Can you give me a hand with clearing the plates, Ethan?'

'Sure.' Ethan rolled his chair away from the table.

'Wait—let us do that for you,' Grayson said, getting to his feet.

'No, absolutely not,' Niamh insisted. 'You're not to make allowances for us. We're quite capable of putting on a dinner party by ourselves. You and Ash can entertain each other for a few minutes. That is, if I can trust you not to be mean to each other.'

'We'll be on our best behaviour,' Grayson said, looking at me with a sardonic glint in his eyes.

'Yes, of course we will,' I said, forcing a smile.

Once Ethan and Niamh had left the room, I picked up my champagne glass and took a sip.

'Aren't you worried you might get another rash from that champagne?' Grayson's expression and tone was playful.

I gave him a mock-glare. 'You could have told me I had beard rash before Niamh noticed it.'

His smile curved one side of his mouth in a way

that was devastatingly attractive. 'I like seeing the effect I have on you. It turns me on.'

I tried but failed to suppress a shiver of reaction. 'Stop it. They might suspect something is going on between us,' I said in a hushed whisper.

He picked up his own glass and took a leisurely sip, his eyes still holding mine. 'What are you doing after you leave here tonight?'

'I'll drive home, take off my make-up, undress, brush my teeth, go to bed. Why?'

His eyes smouldered. 'How about you do all that at my place? We can have a lazy lie-in tomorrow since it's the weekend.'

*A lazy lie-in with Grayson Barlowe.*

Seriously, if anyone had told me only a week or so ago that I would be excited and breathless about such an event I would have told them they were mad. But maybe I was the one who was mad for wanting it so much. I could feel the hot tingle of desire travelling through my body at the thought of sharing Grayson's bed for another night. I had no idea how long our fling was going to last. It could be days or a couple of weeks, tops.

I had to make the most of it, right?

# CHAPTER NINE

I WAS FIRST to wake the following morning and I lay for ages watching Grayson sleep. He was lying on his side, facing me, his eyes closed, his breathing slow and even. I studied each and every one of his features—the long blade of his nose, the dark slashes of his eyebrows above his deep-set eyes, the eyelashes thick and black, the contour of his mouth with its fuller lower lip and the well-defined vermillion borders. His jaw was richly peppered with regrowth and his hair was tousled from both sleep and the play of my fingers during our middle of the night lovemaking.

I shivered as I recalled his urgent possession, the deep and powerful thrusts and the clever flutter of his fingers on my swollen centre that had sent me flying off into the stratosphere. I had to keep reminding myself this was only a fling. That, no matter how wonderful the sex was, it didn't mean our relationship could evolve to anything more lasting. Besides, I wasn't after the fairy tale. I wasn't interested in being someone's wife. Not any more. I had my career and Niamh to focus on. That was more than enough for me…

But in moments like this, with the smell of Grayson on my skin and the taste of him in my mouth, I was tempted…so sorely tempted to dream of more.

Grayson opened his eyes, let out a sleepy sigh and gave a stretch that brought his hair-roughened muscular legs in contact with my smoother ones. 'How long have you been awake?'

'Not long.'

He took a handful of my hair and let it trail through his fingers. 'I can't remember the last time I had a proper lie-in.'

I tiptoed my fingers across the framework of his collarbones. 'What? No lazy lie-ins with your numerous lovers in hotel rooms all over the world? What sort of playboy are you?' I kept my tone light and playful but inside I was hating the thought of him going back to that lifestyle once our fling was over.

Grayson gave a twisted smile that wasn't quite a smile. And there were shadows in his eyes that reminded me of clouds scudding across the wide pavilion of a clear blue sky. His fingers were back in my hair, toying with it as if it was priceless silk he was weighing up whether or not to purchase.

'I'm probably not the most easy-going playboy around. I guess I like being on my own too much.'

I trailed my finger down his sternum, my eyes avoiding his. 'Would you prefer to be alone right now?'

Grayson tipped up my chin with his finger and meshed his gaze with mine. 'No.' There was a definitive quality to his answer that thrilled me to the core.

'I have to warn you, I'm not fully human until I've had caffeine.'

His glinting smile was crooked and did serious damage to the armour around my heart. 'You mean you want me to go downstairs and brew you some coffee before I even kiss you?'

'Well, when you put it like that, I guess one little kiss wouldn't hurt.'

His mouth came down to mine and I forgot all about my need for caffeine. I forgot about everything except the throbbing energy that flowed through my blood as his tongue met mine. His arms gathered me to the warmth of his body, his legs tangling with mine as his kiss deepened. He groaned with pleasure as my hands boldly explored him, the hot satin of his skin and the steel of his arousal exciting me beyond measure.

At the back of my mind, I wondered how I was going to make love to anyone else after Grayson and I ended our fling. Would I even want to? The thought appalled and sickened me. I enjoyed his touch so much; I couldn't imagine wanting anyone like I wanted him.

The sound of a phone ringing by the bedside made Grayson groan in frustration and he lifted his mouth from mine. 'Sorry, I should have turned it onto silent.' He leaned across me to look at the screen, his face screwing up. 'I'd better get this.' He rolled away and sat on the edge of the bed with his back to me. 'Mum?'

I know I shouldn't eavesdrop but it's hard not to hear every word when you're in the same bed as someone receiving a call. Well, that's my excuse and I'm sticking to it.

'Oh, Grayson, I knew something like this would happen,' his mother said. 'If only you and Ash had been a little more positive about Ethan and Niamh getting married.'

I sat up, my heart giving an extra beat at the worried sound of Grayson's mother's voice. Grayson rose from the bed and looked at me.

'What's happened?' he asked in a deceptively calm tone. Deceptively, because I could see the flash of panic in his eyes as they met mine.

'They've eloped,' his mother said.

'Eloped?' Grayson and I said in shocked unison.

There was a beat of awkward silence.

'Is Ash with you?' his mother asked in an equally shocked tone.

I winced and bit my lip. Grayson let out a short breath and answered, 'We're having a breakfast meeting about the house Ethan and Niamh want us to co-design.'

'On a Sunday morning?' his mother asked.

'We're both too busy with our clients during the week,' Grayson said with an eye-roll in my direction. 'Now, what's this about them eloping? We only had dinner with them last night. They can't have gone far.'

'They flew to Vegas first thing this morning.'

'Vegas?' Grayson and I were getting scarily good at the speaking in unison thing.

'Yes, and I blame you both for it. They wanted a lovely church wedding, but you and Ash were so against them even being engaged, they had no choice but to fly to Vegas. I don't even know if their marriage will be legal.'

'Mum, stop panicking. I'll sort it out.' He said a few more reassuring phrases that I barely listened to in my own swirling panic, then he ended the call but kept hold of his phone. 'We have to fly to Vegas and stop them.' He began to scroll on his phone, presumably to book flights.

I was so many steps behind; I was still reeling from the thought of my sister getting married in a Las Vegas chapel instead of the flower-filled church of her dreams. How had I missed the signs that this was what she and Ethan had planned to do? We had shared a meal with them only last night and I had not picked up a single clue that anything like this could happen. But then, I had been totally consumed by my lust for Grayson. I had been so busy trying to hide the truth about our relationship, I hadn't been aware of anything else.

'Fly to Vegas?' I gulped. 'Now?'

'Yes, we have to stop them making the biggest mistake of their lives.'

'But I need to go home and pack.'

'No time. We can buy you some clothes when we get there.'

'I don't have my passport on me.'

'We'll swing by and get it on the way to the airport.'

'But it's close to an eleven-hour flight to Vegas. How will we ever track them down in time?' I asked.

'I'll think of something.'

And by the look of grim determination on his face, I could well believe he could stop a boulder rolling down a mountain.

In a dizzyingly short space of time, we were on a plane to Vegas. I don't remember much about the flight other than my half-hearted attempt to watch a couple of movies. I tried to sleep but the time difference was already messing with my circadian rhythm…or maybe it was Grayson's stern and brooding presence beside me.

'Have you had any success tracking them down? What hotel and so on?' I asked as we came in to land.

'Yep. I tracked Ethan's credit card payments. I've booked us into the same hotel. They only had a six-hour or so start on us, so we should be able to stop them in time.'

'Unless they go straight to the chapel,' I pointed out. 'We're talking about Vegas, remember? I'm pretty sure you can get married at any time of the day or night.'

He glanced at me with a frown. 'Let's hope they have the sense to get over their jetlag before they do such a stupid thing.'

I let a small silence pass.

'Do you think your mother is right? That it's our fault? I mean, we were a little distracted last night.' I bit down on my lower lip, recalling how I had barely touched the lovely food Niamh had gone to so much trouble to prepare. I had been so absorbed by Grayson. Absorbed and bubbling with red-hot desire for him.

He held my gaze and then let out a rough-sounding sigh. 'No, I think they had already planned this—to elope. The payment for the hotel was processed hours before the dinner party.'

It was my turn to frown. 'Oh…'

He lifted my chin to bring my gaze back up to his. 'If this is anyone's fault, it's mine. You warned me from the start about being too against their plans and now look what's happened.'

Look what's happened, indeed. I was fast falling in love with a man I had told myself I hated. I had forbidden myself to think of him as anything but an enemy. A business rival I could not have any connection to, especially in a romantic sense. How could I have been so stupid? So foolish to think I could be immune to him?

I swept the tip of my tongue over my suddenly dry lips. 'We can still stop this. Erm…them, I mean.'

'Can we?' He glanced at my mouth and my stomach hollowed out. His thumb came up and brushed over my lower lip with the softest touch imaginable. 'Maybe some things are unstoppable.' His voice had dropped a couple of semitones, and my spine loosened like molten wax.

I was still trying to think of something to say when his mouth came down and met mine. His lips were feather-light at first but then the pressure increased as desire flared between us like wildfire.

The only thing that brought me back down to earth was the little bump as the plane landed.

Grayson brushed an imaginary hair off my face and gave me a crooked smile. 'Let's see if you're right.'

I couldn't hold back a puzzled frown. 'About what?'

'Let's try and pretend to be positive about Ethan and Niamh's relationship and see what happens.'

'Okay…'

He brushed his thumb across my lower lip again, his expression now cast in shadow. 'I've booked us separate rooms at the hotel, but they're adjoining. I didn't want Ethan and Niamh to know we're involved.'

'Right. Good plan.'

He lifted his finger to my face and smoothed the tiny frown I hadn't even realised was on my forehead. 'Does it make you feel compromised to be lying to your sister?'

'It makes me feel hypocritical.'

His mouth gave a rueful twist. 'Yeah, well, there's that, I guess. Do you want to end it now, before we get to the hotel?'

I couldn't look into his eyes so looked down at my hands in my lap instead.

'Do you?' I tried to make my voice sound casual, light, and not all that invested in how he answered but I couldn't quite pull it off. There was an undercurrent of despair I couldn't disguise, no matter how hard I tried.

He brought my chin up with the tip of his finger, gently turning my face to meet his gaze. 'No.'

'Really?' A bubble of hope rose in my chest. 'I mean, isn't that a little unusual for you, Mr Playboy-About-Town?'

'It is.'

'What do you attribute it to?'

His eyes kindled. 'You.'

'Me?'

His hand cupped one side of my face. 'You make me laugh.'

'What? No one's done that before?'

'Not the way you do.'

I stared at the contours of his mouth, my heart kicking up its pace. It was foolish of me to think he might be falling in love with me. As foolish and idiotic as it was for me to fall for him. But what if he was starting to rethink the timeframe on our fling? We had spent so much time together lately. It didn't feel like a temporary fling at all. It felt like something with the potential to be so much more.

I adopted a teasing expression and met his gaze. 'You'd better go easy on the compliments, or I'll start thinking you'll be booking a chapel as well as your brother.'

A flicker of something passed through his gaze, a slight disturbance like something dark and shadowy moving underneath a deep current of water. 'That's not going to happen.' His tone was adamant but there was a disconnect with the way he was looking at me, as if he was seeing the potential for more and weighing it up in his mind. Or maybe that was my imagination playing tricks on me.

I was saved from having to think of a witty comeback by the disembarking routine. But I was aware of every time Grayson looked at me. Aware of every idle touch of his hand, like when he placed it on the small of my back to guide me down the aisle of the plane. I got the feeling he found it hard to stop himself touching me. I know I found it hard to keep my hands off him. They seemed to gravitate towards him of their own volition. It was like we were programmed now to be physically connected. Our bodies had muscle memory of contact, sensual contact, and wanted more.

Some time later we were in the back of the car he had organised, the driver behind a glass panel, on our way to the hotel. Grayson suddenly glanced at me with an unreadable look. 'You didn't answer my question earlier.'

'Which question was that?'

'On whether you wanted to end our fling now, before we see Ethan and Niamh. You deflected the question back at me without answering it yourself.'

I rolled my lips together, pretending to think about my decision, but I was pretty sure my delay in response wasn't fooling him. 'I think it's okay to continue it for a bit longer.'

'How much longer?'

'How long is a fling or a piece of string?' I quipped back.

His lips moved in the ghost of a smile, but it didn't make the distance to his eyes. 'Funny girl.'

I narrowed my gaze at him in a mock-serious way. 'You're not in danger of falling in love with me, are you?'

The faint disturbance was back in the swirling depths of his gaze. 'Whatever gives you that idea?'

I gave a nonchalant shrug. 'I thought you were always the one to end your flings, but you keep handing me the power to do that. Or are you so confident I'll be like every other woman you've ever dated and beg you to stay with me?'

'Firstly, you're not like anyone else I've dated. And secondly, I'm not going to fall in love with you or anyone.'

I had to act like a veteran thespian to stop myself from revealing how much his words hurt. He was ruling out the possibility of feeling anything for me but lust. His heart was locked away and I wasn't sure I could find the key—or even if there was a key.

'Aren't you worried you might be tempting fate to say that?' I asked with a teasing smile.

'Are you in danger of falling in love with me?' His expression gave nothing away, but I could sense a throb of tension in the air. Or was it fear? The fear of hurting me when that was the last thing he wanted to do. He might have a reputation as a playboy, but he didn't strike me as the sort of man to use women solely as sex objects. He certainly hadn't treated me like that. I had never felt more respected and equal in a sexual relationship before, which made it all the harder to exercise the power to end our fling before I got too attached.

But wasn't I already *too* attached?

# CHAPTER TEN

WE ARRIVED AT the hotel and quickly checked in to our adjoining rooms, both of us keen to track Niamh and Ethan down. Neither of them was responding to calls or text messages, which only ramped up my panic. I couldn't bear the thought of my sister getting married without me there.

Was this *my* fault? Had I driven her to do something she might later regret, only because I was so against her rushing into marriage because, deep down, I was worried about her being hurt? But Ethan was so devoted to her and she to him. Yes, they were still in the heady early days of falling in love, but that didn't mean they couldn't have a lasting relationship. I had allowed my cynicism about relationships to influence my judgement, but what sort of authority did I have over being in love? I hadn't been in love with Ryan. I realised now I had settled for second best because it made me feel less guilty about Niamh's situation. My distorted thinking had been: how could I allow myself to fall properly in love if she never found someone herself?

But Niamh had found someone and with zero help from me. And if I didn't get there in time, she would marry him in a Vegas chapel instead of the flower-filled village church of her dreams.

Grayson and I made our way to the chapel situated in the hotel, our pace brisk and determined.

'Let's hope we can catch them in time,' he said, frowning heavily.

'Yes, but if we don't, I think we have to be as positive as we can. The last thing any couple wants on their wedding day is negativity.' I blew out a breath and added, 'I can't help blaming myself for this. I shouldn't have been so against them being together.'

Grayson sent me a sideways glance as we traversed another long, garishly carpeted corridor. 'If anyone's to blame, it's me. I hated the thought of Ethan going through another heartbreak.'

We came to the chapel before I could think of a response. Another couple was stepping away from the marriage celebrant, their faces wreathed in smiles. And next in line were Niamh and Ethan. I allowed myself a moment of relief to sweep through me before stepping forward with Grayson. At least they weren't yet married.

Niamh turned her head as we approached and glared at us. 'You can't stop us.'

'We don't want to stop you,' Grayson said in a calm and measured tone. 'We want you to do it properly, at home surrounded by friends and family.'

'Really?' Ethan said, with a surprised look.

'Of course,' I chipped in. 'This isn't the wedding day you've always dreamed of, Niamh. Let us at least give you both a wedding day to remember.'

Niamh exchanged a glance with Ethan before turning back to me. 'But we want to get married sooner rather than later,' she said, lowering her gaze from mine and chewing at her lip.

My sister was never all that good at delaying gratification, but who was I to talk? I had rushed into a fling with Grayson because I couldn't help myself. He was temptation personified.

'I'm sure we can organise a lovely wedding in a few weeks,' I said.

'No, we d-don't want to w-wait a few weeks,' Ethan said, stumbling over his words in his haste to get them out in a determined tone.

'Don't weddings take ages to organise?' Grayson asked.

'Yes, but I know of a good wedding planner that might be able to help,' I said. 'There's a company run by three best friends called Happy Ever After Weddings. I've read about their hugely successful business and seen interviews on various social platforms. But, of course, they are popular, so it might not be easy to engage them, especially with such a short timeframe.'

'Can we talk in private?' Niamh asked me with a beseeching glance.

'Sure, but you'd better tell the celebrant we won't be needing them,' I said.

Ethan and Niamh mumbled something to the celebrant, who didn't seem all that fussed with the sudden change of plan. But, judging from the queue of couples lining up to get married, perhaps he was confident the vacant space would be filled within minutes.

I took my sister by the hand and led her out of the chapel. I spied a café nearby and suggested we go there.

'No, I want somewhere more private,' Niamh said.

'Okay, we'll go to my room.' I led the way to the lift.

'You have your own room?' Niamh asked once we were inside the lift and zooming up to the thirtieth floor.

'Of course.'

Her forehead creased in a puzzled frown. 'But I thought you might share with Grayson.'

I could feel heat pooling in my cheeks. Not

could I only feel it, but I could also see it because three sides of the lift were mirrored glass.

I gave a little cough of a laugh. 'Why on earth would you think that?'

'I see the way he looks at you. And the way you look at him.'

'Erm…well, he's… I'm…' What was I supposed to say? How could I explain our fling to my sister? What sort of hypocrite would she think me?

'Are you in love with him?'

I rapid blinked like I was a rabbit suddenly realising a speeding car was about to turn me into roadkill. Niamh's question blindsided me. I didn't want to think about my feelings for Grayson Barlowe. I didn't want to acknowledge I even had feelings for him. We were having a lust-fuelled fling. Emotions were not supposed to be part of the deal.

'Erm…it's complicated…' What a pathetic cliché to resort to, but it was actually true. It didn't get much more complicated. 'So, what did you want to talk to me about?' It was time to get the focus back on her, not me.

Now it was time for Niamh's cheeks to go pink. 'Let's wait until we're in your room.'

The lift doors pinged open, and we stepped out and made our way to my room. I glanced at Grayson's door next to mine and a hot shiver passed through my body.

I opened the door to my room and Niamh

walked through. I closed the door and followed her to the sitting room that overlooked the colourful and busy Vegas Strip.

'So, what did you want to talk to me about?' I asked.

Niamh turned from looking out of the window, her hands twisted together in front of her body. 'I'm having a baby.'

I stared at her in shocked silence. My mind was spinning out of control like a Buick on black ice. Niamh was pregnant? She was going to be a mother. Ethan was going to be a father. I was going to be an auntie. Grayson was going to be an uncle.

'Aren't you going to say something?' Niamh was looking a little worried.

I blew out an uneven breath. 'Wow... I mean... congratulations. How many weeks?'

'Four.'

'Four?' I gaped at her. 'But you only started seeing each other, what, seven weeks ago now?' That meant she'd got pregnant at the very start of their relationship.

'Yes, but our connection was instant. I knew he was the love of my life the minute I met him.'

I sat down because my legs were suddenly strangely unsteady. 'Wow, I can see why you both wanted to get married in a rush.'

I shook my head, trying to get my brain around this new development. There was so much to think about. How would my sister cope with the responsibilities that came with motherhood? Our own mother hadn't had any of the limitations Niamh had and she had really struggled with the day in, day out routine of providing for and taking care of her children.

'Aren't you happy for me?'

I painted a bright smile on my face and sprang to my feet and enveloped her in a hug. 'Of course I am. I'm thrilled for you and Ethan.'

Niamh finally stepped out of my embrace and beamed at me. 'Ethan will be the most wonderful father. He's so excited because he never thought he would have the opportunity. I know there'll be obstacles to face but I'm sure we'll face them together.'

I wasn't sure what Grayson would think of this new development. He was far more against their wedding than I was, and I was pretty determined against it. Now I couldn't wait for them to tie the knot.

But not here.

Not in Las Vegas.

Half an hour later, Niamh left to go back to her and Ethan's room to pack for the trip home. I had already emailed Happy Ever After Weddings and as soon as the time difference and travel distance allowed I would call into their London office in person. I didn't care how much it cost but my sister was going to have the wedding of her dreams.

There was a tap at my door, and I opened it to find Grayson standing there with a grim look on his face.

'You know?'

'Yes, Ethan told me.' He stepped through and I closed the door behind him.

'I hope you weren't too negative about it.'

He scraped his hand through his hair and let out a whooshing breath. 'This changes everything. My mother is going to be beside herself with joy.'

'And you? Are you excited about being an uncle?'

I studied his features, wondering what was going on behind the screen of his shuttered gaze.

'I haven't given it much thought. What about you?'

I rolled my lips together, not sure how to answer. I was still trying to get my head around my sister becoming a mother. She had always been my little sister, the person who depended on me for everything. But, in the space of weeks, I had been cast aside for her fiancé. Now they were going to be parents. So many changes in such a short timeframe.

'On one level I'm thrilled to be an auntie, but on another I'm worried how my sister will cope with all the responsibilities of motherhood.'

'Yes, well, every new parent goes on a steep learning curve, from what I've heard. But I'm sure Ethan will support her in every way he can. And my mother, of course.'

There was a beat or two of silence where we just stood looking at each other.

I couldn't read his expression and I desperately hoped he couldn't read mine. I was trying to hide my emotions. The emotions I wasn't supposed to be feeling. The emotions I had forbidden myself to feel. But I was feeling them all the same.

I'm not sure how it happened but I was in love with him. I loved so much about him. The way he supported and protected his brother, the way he worked hard at his career, the values he stood by and his strength of character and self-discipline.

And I loved how he made love to me.

'I've booked a flight for us all,' Grayson said. 'The sooner we get back to London the better.'

'You're right. It's going to take a miracle to get a wedding organised in a couple of weeks.'

Grayson stepped up close, so our toes were almost touching. He lifted a hand to my face and stroked the curve of my cheek with a lazy finger. 'I wish we had more time.'

'For?'

He leaned down so his mouth was just above mine. 'For this.' His lips covered mine and I was swept up in the magic of the moment. No one had ever kissed me with such tender thoroughness. No one had ever made my blood sing in my veins the way he did. It was a kiss that spoke of fervent passion and deep longing. I wound my arms around his neck, my body pressed close to the strong wall of his. I could not bear to think of a time when I wouldn't be able to do this—to be so close to him I could feel the thunder of his heart against me.

Grayson finally lifted his mouth off mine and gave me a twisted smile. 'Hold that thought until we get back to London.'

I ran my hands down his chest and let them settle on his trim waist. 'I think Niamh suspects we're seeing each other.'

A flicker of something passed through his gaze. 'How? Did you say something to her?'

'No, but she noticed how you look at me.'

He frowned. 'How do I look at you?'

'The same way I look at you.'

He brushed the pad of his thumb across my lower lip, sending my senses into a tailspin. 'I guess it's hard to hide the sort of chemistry we have.'

I eased myself out of his arms. 'Yes, well, it's not going to last for ever, is it? These things have a habit of burning out over time.' I spoke with cool detachment but inside I was thinking the opposite. I knew it was not going to burn out for me.

How could it when I loved him with every fibre of my being?

His jaw tightened as if he was thinking over an appropriate response. His expression was mask-like but I could sense movement at the back of his gaze.

'Is it burning out for you?' His tone was as cool and detached as mine.

'Not yet.'

His gaze lowered to my mouth and the floor of my belly shivered. 'Good to know.' His hands settled on my hips and he brought me a tiny bit closer. I could feel the press of his erection and my pulse began to quicken.

'Don't we have a flight to catch?' My voice was shamefully breathless, my skin tightening all over with desire.

'It's a private flight—it won't matter if we're five minutes late.'

'Five minutes? You reckon you can get me to come that quickly?'

He gave me a wolfish smile and brought his mouth down closer to mine. 'Watch me.'

The next couple of weeks were nothing short of a whirlwind of activity. I had to juggle work with dress fittings and meetings with the team at Happy Ever After Weddings, who had kindly taken Niamh and Ethan on, due to another couple postponing their wedding due to the groom injuring himself in an accident.

It was so different from when I had planned my own wedding. For one thing, I hadn't been anywhere near as excited and happy as Niamh. I hadn't been glowing with love for my fiancé. I had simply been going through the motions, ticking the boxes that needed to be ticked. Find dress. *Tick*. Book church. *Tick*. Select reception venue and menu. *Tick*. It had been a long list of jobs to get done.

Witnessing my sister's joy and anticipation made me feel increasingly envious. I began to daydream about my fling with Grayson becoming something else. Something more lasting. Something that would lead us to plan a wedding one day. I could imagine my joy and excitement if I was engaged to Grayson. I could imagine wearing his ring and looking at him the way my sister looked at his brother.

I could even imagine carrying Grayson's child.

I placed a hand on my belly, as I had seen my sister do so many times over the last couple of weeks. What would it feel like to have Grayson's child in my womb? I pushed the thought away before it could get a stronger foothold. What was I doing? I was a career woman through and through. I didn't have time for kids. My career was too front and centre. So too was my commitment to Niamh. I had always put her before everything.

*But Niamh has Ethan now.*

The thought was reassuring and yet…and yet I was so used to being there for my sister. I didn't know any other way of living. For the last twenty years I had been there for her. I had overseen her education, her medical care, her social life—her everything.

Who was I without her needing me?

In amongst all the wedding preparations, Grayson and I were still meeting after hours to work on Ethan and Niamh's house design. Neither of us had told our siblings about our relationship but I was feeling increasingly uncomfortable about the secrecy.

It was Grayson's turn to come to my house a couple of days before the wedding. I opened the door to him, and he stepped inside and closed the door. He reached for me and dropped a firm kiss to my lips. 'I've missed you.'

I leaned back in his embrace to look up at him. 'But you saw me the day before yesterday.'

His arms tightened around me, and my pulse began to gallop. 'I like seeing you every day.' His voice was husky and low, his gaze dark and glittering.

'I like seeing you too.' I stood on tiptoe to plant a kiss on his lips.

He groaned and pulled me even closer, his mouth taking charge. His tongue slipped between my lips and danced with mine. Heat exploded in my body, my legs trembling, my spine loosening, my heart racing. We stumbled to my bedroom, knocking against furniture as we went, our mouths glued together as the passion between us soared. It was always like this—a rush of desire that was so heady it made me dizzy. I could not get enough of this man's touch.

'I want you,' I said.

'I want you more.'

I smiled against the sensual texture of his lips. 'Prove it.'

And so he did.

# CHAPTER ELEVEN

THE DAY OF Niamh and Ethan's wedding arrived and, miracle of miracles, it was a sunny day. As I was Niamh's bridesmaid and Grayson was Ethan's best man, he was standing at the altar with his brother in his chair beside him as I preceded Niamh up the aisle. The music was emotionally evocative, and I had to blink to keep the tears back.

I locked gazes with Grayson and my heart skipped a beat. He was looking at me with such glittering intensity, as if he was committing the vision of me in my silk shell-pink bridesmaid dress to memory. I could feel his eyes on every curve of my body—curves he had caressed with his hands and his lips and tongue only the night before.

Niamh had chosen to walk herself up the aisle, which was another sign of how she was growing more and more independent of me. I was proud of her and yet a little sad too. I was so accustomed to being included in every part of her life but now she had Ethan and he would be her mainstay, not me.

The church was awash with flowers and the fragrance was intoxicating. Niamh looked exactly as a bride should look—beautiful and happy beyond description. And Ethan looked exactly as a groom should look—proud and desperately in love. The ceremony was traditional, and I didn't bother disguising my tears at one point. The exchange of vows was so meaningful, and I had no doubt that this couple, in spite of all the obstacles they had faced in life to this point, would be happy and stay happy. For ever.

If only I could have the same with Grayson.

The church bells rang as the couple left the church. Grayson and I followed in their wake, and I was conscious of my shoulder brushing against his arm as we walked back down the aisle.

'You look very beautiful,' he said.

'Thank you. I wasn't sure about the colour on me, but Niamh insisted on it.'

Grayson smiled and my heart did a somersault. 'Are you wearing underwear under it?'

'No.'

His eyes smouldered and he gave a low and deep groan. 'You shouldn't have told me that.'

'But you asked.'

'I'm not going to be able to think of anything else now.'

'Careful. Some people can lipread, you know.' I smiled at the people in the congregation as we walked past them to the bright sunlight outside the church.

'Just wait until I get you alone.'

'Promises, promises,' I said in a sing-song voice.

The sunlight was blinding, so too were Ethan and Niamh's smiles as they greeted their guests.

Grayson's mother, Julie, came up to me, beaming with happiness. 'Wasn't it the most beautiful ceremony? I was crying buckets as soon as I saw Niamh. I'm so glad you supported her and Ethan in their relationship. And I'm so grateful you talked Grayson round.'

'I didn't really talk him round.'

'Don't be so modest. Of course you did,' she said, glancing at Grayson, who was a few feet away. 'He can be so very stubborn, but somehow you got him to change his mind.' She swung her gaze back to me. 'Anyway, it's lovely to have a daughter-in-law at last. And I'm so excited about the baby.'

'Yes, so am I.'

I did my level best not to look at Grayson. I was trying so hard to appear indifferent to him, but every time I happened to glance in his direction I found his gaze on me.

'So, you and Grayson will have to be friends

now,' Julie said. 'We can't have the baby's uncle and auntie not liking each other, now, can we?'

'I'm sure we'll manage to be civil to one another when required,' I said with an on-off smile.

Julie studied Grayson for a moment, then turned back to me. 'I can't help thinking he's changed lately.'

'How so?'

'He's happier, more at ease. Or maybe that's because Ethan is finally settled with the love of his life.' She gave a sad little smile and continued, 'Grayson has always blamed himself for the accident.'

'It's hard not to feel guilty when things happen on your watch.'

'I heard about Niamh's accident. That must have been so hard on you.' Her empathetic tone was almost my undoing. Almost.

'It was...' I had to blink away another prickle of tears. 'It is...'

Julie put a gentle hand on my arm. 'It probably always will be. But it doesn't mean you can't move forward. Don't let the past dictate your future.'

I didn't get the chance to reply, even if I could have thought of a thing to say. The photographer directed the wedding party to assemble for the official photographs. Once they were taken and refreshments were being handed around, Grayson came over to me.

'How are you holding up?'

'My feet are killing me and my face aches from all the smiling.'

'I hope my mother wasn't too full-on,' he said.

'She was lovely.'

He grunted and swung his gaze to look at Ethan and Niamh, surrounded by the other guests. 'As long as she didn't put any ideas into your head.'

I stiffened. 'What ideas do you mean?'

He turned back to me and gave a careless shrug, his expression masked. 'Weddings do strange things to people. Make them get all sentimental.'

I wasn't going to admit to how sentimental I was feeling but I needed to counter-argue on principle. 'I don't think it's strange to feel sentimental at a wedding. It's kind of nice to see two people who love each other make a public commitment.'

He thrust his hands in his pockets and gazed again at the assembled guests sipping champagne and eating canapés. 'Most people fall out of love before the honeymoon is over.'

'Don't be so cynical. Some people fall in love and stay in love for a lifetime.'

He glanced at me with an unreadable expression. 'I thought you were as cynical as me. What's happened?'

'Nothing. I just think there are other ways of looking at things.'

I saw Ethan and Niamh approaching at that point and I hastily painted a smile on my face. 'I don't think I've ever seen a more blissfully happy couple. Congratulations. It was an exquisitely beautiful wedding.'

Ethan's arm went around Niamh's waist, his expression so full of love as he looked up at her from his chair it was enough to make my heart contract. If only Grayson would look at me like that. Or was I wishing for the moon?

'We should have made it a double wedding,' Niamh said, grinning at us.

'What?' Grayson barked the word, clearly shocked by my sister's comment.

I was a little shocked too. Shocked that she had put two and two together in spite of my efforts to keep my relationship with Grayson a secret.

'Don't be silly, Niamh,' I said with a laugh that sounded tinny.

Niamh was undaunted by our reaction. 'You can't fool us. We know you've been together for ages. You don't have to hide it from us. There's nothing to be ashamed of in falling in love.'

'We're not in love,' Grayson said in a tone that was so adamant I couldn't help but feel crushed.

Niamh looked confused and glanced at me. 'But I don't understand…'

'No, you're the ones who don't understand,' Grayson said. 'It's not going to happen.'

'What's not g-going to happen?' Ethan asked, frowning.

'This.' Grayson waved his hand to encompass the church in the background and the assembled guests in the garden. 'Any marriage between us is out of the question.'

I was determined not to sabotage my sister's wedding day by demonstrating how hurt I was by Grayson's stance, but it called on every bit of acting ability I possessed.

'That's right,' I said. 'We had a little fling but it's over now.'

'Over?' Niamh and Ethan spoke in unison.

Grayson said nothing, showed nothing. It was like someone had poured invisible concrete over him, freezing him in place.

'Yes, over, but we're friends,' I said. 'And we're both looking forward to being uncle and auntie to your baby.'

Some other guests came over to speak to the bride and groom and I was immensely glad of the chance to escape. But I had only got as far as the lychgate when I felt a strong hand come down on my arm.

'Wait. I want to talk to you.'

I turned to look up at Grayson's frowning features. 'What's there to talk about? You've made it perfectly clear you see no future for us.'

He let out a breath and a curse word at the same time. 'We agreed on a fling.'

'Yes, and now it's over.'

'But I don't want it to be over.' The words seemed to be forced out of him, as if he had not wanted to admit his continued desire for me.

I shook his hand off my arm. 'It has to be over, Grayson. You know it does. I'm getting too involved with you. I don't want to get hurt.'

'How will I hurt you?'

I gave a sad smile. 'By not loving me.'

His brows snapped together, and his expression became guarded. 'Are you saying you love me?'

I so wanted to deny it. I could taste the word 'no' on the tip of my tongue. It was teetering there like a skier at the top of a steep run, poised, waiting to fly down. But I couldn't say it. I was tired of pretending. Tired of pretending to be someone I wasn't. I had done it for years, fashioning myself into a person I could barely recognise as myself any more. It was time to be honest about what I wanted, what I hoped for, what I deserved but had denied myself out of guilt.

'Yes, I do love you. I know we agreed to keep our feelings out of it, but I couldn't do it. You made it so hard for me by being everything I didn't even know I wanted in a partner. I started to realise I wanted what Niamh has. Someone to love her and be with her through whatever life dishes out. All this time, I've been thinking she was too immature, too inexperienced to handle marriage, but it's me that needed to grow up. Continuing our fling when there's no possibility of it ever being anything but a fling would be wrong for me on so many levels.'

Grayson's expression underwent a series of changes as I spoke. Shock. Distress. A flicker of anger. A stiffening of his features that looked like a drawbridge was being pulled up inside him. 'So, that's it? You want to end it?'

'It's for the best.'

'Do I get a say in this?'

I swallowed a thickness in my throat. 'Sure, but nothing you say will change my mind. Unless you were to say you love me and want a future with me. A future that included marriage and hopefully kids one day.'

'I've never wanted those things with anyone.'

'I know. You were nothing if not brutally honest with me.'

'Then why did you fall in love with me?'

I gave a frustrated laugh that wasn't really a laugh. 'Because you have so much to offer. You're a good person, Grayson. A strong and capable person who takes his responsibilities seriously. Everything you do, you do to a high standard. And no one has ever made me feel the way you do physically. I know sex isn't everything in a relationship but it's a pretty good barometer. But physical chemistry isn't enough. You won't allow yourself to love anyone because of what happened to Ethan. Guilt has tortured you as it has tortured me. But I'm not going to live my life under that dark cloud, pretending I don't want the things I really do want. I want the fairy tale that you don't even believe in, even when it's right in front of you.'

He paced back and forth until I was sure he was going to wear out the grass beneath his feet. His agitation was palpable, it made the atmosphere crackle like an approaching storm.

He suddenly stopped pacing and his eyes cut to mine, his mouth pulled tight. 'This is not how I saw us ending.'

'I know, because you're the one who's usually in control of your flings. Doesn't that tell you something? You need to be in control because it's too threatening to give others the power to hurt you.'

'You haven't hurt me. You've surprised me.'

I folded my arms across my middle. I was so tempted to cave in and go back to him. Every cell of my body was drawn to him as if pulled by an invisible force. But I had to be strong. I had to summon every bit of willpower in order to complete my journey as a fully evolved human being. No more self-denial. No more pretending. No more bending myself out of shape to be someone I was not destined to be.

'I really want us to be friends, Grayson. There are other people who will get hurt if we're not.'

His top lip gave the tiniest curl as if he couldn't help himself, and his eyes glittered with his trademark cynicism. 'You expect me to greet you with a chaste kiss on the cheek after you've come apart so many times in my arms? Just to give you the heads-up—that's what I'll be thinking every time I see you.'

I raised my chin a fraction, even as my traitorous body throbbed and throbbed with longing. 'You'll have dozens, if not hundreds, of lovers after me. I'm sure you'll forget all about our time together.'

He grunted something unintelligible, his expression brooding. 'Why end it today of all days? Why not wait until tomorrow?'

'Because Ethan and Niamh's wedding vows really spoke to me,' I said. 'Every word was so meaningful. The promises they made to each other are promises I want to make to the man I love. That man is you, Grayson, but you can't love anyone because, deep down, you don't like yourself. You've not forgiven yourself for letting Ethan drive that night. Until you can accept you are human, just like everyone else, and that making mistakes is part and parcel of the human condition, then I don't think you will ever be truly content, much less happy. Part of the reason you work so hard is to fill in the empty spaces in your life. I've done it too, for so long I thought it was part of my true nature. But while I love my work, I can no longer be a slave to it and allow it to crowd out some of the most important things a human being can experience—connection, commitment, and lasting love.'

'Thanks for the free psychotherapy session, but I'm quite content with my life as it is.' His voice was cold and distant, his expression closed-off.

'You might be now, but what about in a few years' time? How long do you think you can move from casual lover to casual lover, never staying with them long enough to get to know them or for them to get to know you? How long is that going to be satisfying?'

Grayson moved away a short distance to rest his hands on top of the wooden fence that divided the churchyard from a park. He stared at the trees waving in the slight breeze, every muscle on his face taut with tension.

'Okay, you've said your piece. I understand you want more, but I did warn you from the beginning there wasn't going to be more.'

'I know you did.' I let out a wobbly breath and walked back to the other guests.

I was trying so hard to hold it together, trying so hard to be strong and dignified, but inside I wanted to shout, I wanted to scream, I wanted to beg him to love me. It was strange to be on the opposite side of a breakup. I was the one who had broken off my engagement to Ryan. Looking back now, I could have done things a little more graciously, allowed him some measure of dignity, but my protective instincts towards Niamh had taken over. I hadn't been in love with Ryan, and I suspect he might not have been in love with me either.

But I was in love with Grayson. He was everything I could ever want in a life partner. He totally understood my commitment to my sister because he had the same commitment to his brother. He understood the guilt I carried because he had experienced the same. During our fling I had started to hope he was developing an attachment to me that was deeper and more enduring than his past casual encounters. That I was someone special.

Clearly, I was wrong.

I wasn't anything special to Grayson Barlowe. I was just another lover, just another woman who had succumbed to his potent charm.

And now it was over.

I don't know how I got through the rest of Niamh and Ethan's wedding day. The reception seemed to drag on for hours…or maybe that was because I was doing my best to avoid Grayson. But escaping him was impossible because, as best man and the only bridesmaid, we each had roles to play.

One of those roles included stepping up on the dance floor to join the bride and groom in their first dance together. I stepped into Grayson's embrace and tried to block my body's reaction, but it was like trying to stop a wave from cresting. A rush of longing flowed through me, a deep and unsettling longing because I knew it could not be satiated. Not now. Not ever again. We had done many things together before, intimate things that were etched on my mind and my body, but we had never danced before. How bittersweet to realise we were so well matched in this way too. We moved together as if we had been dancing partners for years. It felt so natural and easy to glide with him across the floor. I breathed in his smell, committing it to memory, for I knew I might never have the chance to get this close to him again. In a way, our dance was a goodbye and that made it especially poignant.

Other couples had joined us and the dance floor was a little more crowded, so Grayson had to hold me closer to avoid any collisions. I was aware of the gentle press of his hand in the small of my back, aware of how close our hips were, aware of the grasp of his hand and how my hand was so small and dainty inside the firm cage of his.

'Ash…' There was a strange quality to his voice, a slight hitch in it that I had not heard before.

I looked up at him to find his gaze on me, a frown etched on his forehead.

'Yes?' I tried to remove the note of hope in my tone but I'm sure he could see it in my face. I'm a good actor, but not *that* good.

His eyes dipped to my mouth for a long moment and my heart skittered. 'Is it going to be difficult for you to work with me on Ethan and Niamh's house? If so, I can organise one of my staff to take over the project for me.'

I frowned. I had forgotten about the house we were supposed to be designing together. We hadn't got far with it, mostly because of the wedding taking up so much of our time recently. How would it be working alongside him now we weren't seeing each other any more? It would be torture, that's what it would be. Plain and simple emotional and physical torture.

'But they want us to do it. I'm sure we can both be grown-ups about this.'

One side of his mouth tilted in a half smile that didn't reach his eyes. 'You think I won't be able to control myself around you?'

'I'm sure you'll be the ultimate professional at all times.'

He held my gaze for a heart-stopping moment

before looking away into the distance. 'We'd better reinstate the no-touching rule.'

'Fine.'

'And that probably should include earrings.'

In spite of my heartache, I laughed. 'I'll wear
studs, so you won't be tempted.'

He looked back at me again, his eyes dark and
intense. 'I only have to look at you to be tempted.'
His voice was rough around the edges and his hold
on me momentarily tightened, sending waves of
incendiary heat through my body.

I aimed my gaze at his bowtie, not trusting myself to look into those mesmerising eyes. But I
was acutely aware of how close our pelvises were
to each other. It seemed our bodies gravitated to
each other of their own volition, like two magnets
locking together.

'You have to stop looking at me like that,' I said,
keeping my voice low so the other couples dancing around us wouldn't hear.

'How am I looking at you?'

'Like you want to whisk me away and make
love to me.'

'But that's exactly what I want to do.'

'But you can't, not now. We're over.' I injected
my voice with as much determination as I could.

'You really think you can turn off feelings just
like that?'

I glanced up at him, my heart climbing up to

my throat. 'But we're not talking about feelings, or at least you're not. Our fling was never about feelings for you. It was about lust. And yes, that can be turned off if you're strong enough.' I only hoped I was strong enough, otherwise the next few months, or even years, were going to be hard to get through.

He frowned and looked into the distance again but his hold on me remained firm. 'Why are you so sure you love me? What if you're confusing it with lust?'

'I know this is probably hard for you to understand because you won't allow your feelings to get involved in your flings, but as soon as you kissed me I knew I was in danger of falling in love with you. But it wasn't just about the physical chemistry. Your character spoke to me in a way no one else has before. You understood my struggles because you had experienced them yourself. I felt like you were seeing me, the real me, instead of the persona I've adopted over the years. I could be myself with you and I like to think you could be yourself with me.'

I don't know how it happened, but we were no longer on the dance floor and had drifted out to a balcony festooned with flowers. There was no one else out there, so we were finally alone.

Grayson lowered his hands from my body and stepped back a step, his expression as inscrutable as the stone wall to our left. 'It was never my intention to hurt you.' His voice contained a chord of gravitas that made me realise this was painful for him too, for different reasons but painful regardless. I knew it wasn't in his nature to be cruel. Cynical, yes, but not cruel.

I painted on a brave smile. 'I'll get over it.'

He stepped closer again and gently stroked my cheek with a lazy finger, his eyes locking on mine. 'Will you?'

'Of course.' I wasn't as confident as I sounded. Inside, my heart was breaking like a fissure in a rock.

'Am I allowed one last kiss?' The rough burr of his voice sent a shiver down the length of my spine.

'Do you think that's wise?' My voice was not much above a whisper and my pulse began to pound.

Grayson's eyes moved back and forth between each of mine, and then his gaze lowered to my mouth for a pulse-tripping moment. He slowly brushed the pad of his thumb across my lower lip, and I trembled from head to foot.

His mouth twisted into a rueful line and his hand fell away to drop by his side. 'You're right. It's not at all wise.' And then he turned and walked away without another word.

# CHAPTER TWELVE

THE NEXT MONTH I spent catching up on work. I had a lot of clients on the go and a couple of big new projects that took up a great deal of time. But my work was no longer as satisfying as it had been. Or maybe it was because I had no work/life balance. I worked all day and came home to an empty house. I didn't socialise because I didn't have the energy or the motivation. I missed Niamh but I was happy she was enjoying her new life with Ethan.

And it goes without saying I missed Grayson.

I missed his touch, his rare smiles, his intelligent conversation—so many things that made him so attractive to me. I missed hearing the sound of his voice, I missed the smell of him on my skin, the taste of him in my mouth, the feel of his arms so protective and strong around me.

We hadn't yet met up to continue working on Niamh and Ethan's house. I had been too busy with other clients, and I heard via Ethan that Grayson was snowed under with work too. He also told me Grayson had flown to the US to check on a build that was part-way done. I tortured myself with imagining him hooking up with someone over there. No doubt he would go back to his playboy lifestyle and barely spare me a thought.

But a couple of days later I was helping Niamh shop for baby things, and she told me Ethan was worried about Grayson.

'Why?' I asked, picking up a lemon-coloured onesie.

'He thinks Grayson's not himself at all.'

I put the onesie down and picked up a tiny bonnet and mittens, trying to disguise my avid interest in Grayson's state of mind. Trying too to disguise how envious I was of my sister shopping for babywear. Would I ever have the chance to do the same? I couldn't imagine having anyone else's child than Grayson's. But he didn't want the things I wanted.

He didn't want me. Not for ever.

'He's grumpy and unsociable,' Niamh said, handing me a bundle of clothes to hold. 'He won't come over for dinner and he won't allow us to visit him. Even their mum is worried about him.' She looked at me with her big blue eyes and asked, 'Did you part as friends or as enemies?'

'Friends... I think...' I bent down to pick up one of the onesies that dropped to the floor and added it back to the tower of items I was trying to juggle in my arms. How could one small baby need all this stuff? I tried to think of the last time I had held a baby, but I couldn't remember doing so since I was a teenager. Now all I could think about was holding one of my own. Why was I torturing myself with these thoughts? It was pointless. Grayson was not going to change his mind. He had made his position crystal-clear, and I had to put my big girl panties on and accept it.

Niamh started sorting through some christening outfits hanging on a rack. 'Ethan and I have tweaked a few of our ideas for our house. Maybe you and Grayson could get together soon to go over them.' She glanced at me over her shoulder and added, 'Or will that be too awkward for you now you're only…friends?'

I fashioned my lips into a confident smile, but it was totally at odds with how I was feeling. I didn't know how I was going to be in the same room as Grayson without wanting to touch him. How could I work alongside him for months and not embarrass myself by begging him to reconsider?

'It won't be a problem.'

Niamh selected a long white, beautifully embroidered christening gown and held it up for me to see. 'What do you think?'

I reached out and touched the finely embroidered fabric, thinking of the little person who would wear it in a few months' time—my niece or nephew. It looked like a family heirloom, the sort of gown generations of babies could wear. Would I ever have a baby to wear it? Or would I always feel this crushing sense of loneliness and emptiness because the only man I could ever love didn't love me back?

'It's gorgeous.'

She lowered the gown to look directly at me. 'Ethan and I want you and Grayson to be our baby's godparents.'

I tried not to show my sense of unease. Not because I didn't want to be a godparent—it was an incredible honour, and I wouldn't dream of declining. But it would be yet another permanent connection with Grayson. How was I going to avoid him when there would be so many events where we would both be present?

'Oh, that's so lovely of you both. I'd be honoured, of course.'

Niamh beamed and added the christening gown to the pile of clothes I was already balancing in my arms. 'That's settled then. Now, let's have tea and cake.'

I know what you're thinking. I don't drink tea, right? But guess what? Ever since I broke up with Grayson, I haven't been able to bring myself to drink coffee. I can't even bear the smell because it reminds me too much of him.

Speaking of smells—I still have his handkerchief. I know I can get a little preachy about always returning things you've borrowed but I kept hold of Grayson's handkerchief, even though I'd had numerous opportunities to return it before I ended our fling. I'd washed and ironed it and now I kept it under my pillow. I find myself reaching for it each night, clutching it in my hand like a child clutches a favourite toy. Pathetic, right?

The following Friday I went straight home after work rather than join my team for end-of-the-week drinks. I wasn't in the mood for socialising, and I found it hard to make small talk because my life was so boring compared to everyone else's. All I did these days was work and exercise. Okay, I lied about the exercise. If you can call running ten metres along the platform to catch the Tube three mornings this week exercise, well, I tick the box. The other thing I hated when going out was seeing all the other couples. It was like rubbing rock salt into the open wound of my broken heart. Why was everyone so damn happy when I was so utterly miserable?

I picked at some leftovers for dinner but ended up pushing it away with a sigh. I surfed the streaming platforms on my smart television but, in spite of the huge number of options, nothing appealed to me in this bleak mood.

I sat on my window seat and looked at the street

below. More couples walking hand in hand, families taking the kids and the dog for a walk. A young couple taking their baby for a stroll in one of those old-fashioned prams with large springs and shiny spoked wheels. And elderly couple walking hand in hand. A tall dark-haired man with a slight limp, carrying a bunch of flowers, walking on his own…

I sat upright, my eyes narrowing to focus on that all too familiar figure. My mouth dried, my stomach flip-flopped, my pulse hammered.

The man looked up and locked gazes with me and my heart went into arrythmia. He gave a slow smile and I rose from the seat on legs as unsteady as a newborn foal's. It could only have been seconds before my doorbell rang but it felt like a decade.

I took a calming breath, not wanting to get ahead of myself, but it was hard to control the leaping of my pulse and the balloon of hope rising in my chest. I opened the door and Grayson Barlowe was standing there with a beautiful bunch of sweet peas in his hand.

'Hi…' I said, my nerves making my voice sound gruff rather than welcoming.

'Hi. May I come in?' His eyes had a light in them I had not seen before. A light that sparkled and shone and made him seem younger and less burdened than he had been in the past.

'Sure.' I stepped back and he came through the door, bringing his alluring scent with him, sending me into an instant swoon.

Grayson handed me the fragrant sweet peas. 'These are for you.'

'Thank you.' I took them from him and buried my face in the colourful sweet-smelling blooms. 'Mmm…these are my absolute favourite.' I raised my gaze to his. 'A lucky guess?'

His wry smile made my heart skip a beat. 'Niamh happened to mention you like them.'

'Come through,' I said with an on-off smile. 'I'll put these in some water.'

He followed me into my kitchen and I made a business of finding a vase, filling it with water and arranging the sweet peas. I was aware of him watching me the whole time, but I tried not to show how much his presence affected me.

'So, have Ethan and Niamh mentioned the god-parent thing?' I asked, placing the vase of sweet peas in the middle of the kitchen table.

'Yes.'

I turned to look at him. 'It's a big honour. I've never been one before, have you?'

'No, but there's a first time for everything, right?' There was a definite twinkle in his eye and his tone was playful.

'Right.'

He came a little closer and I snatched in an even

breath. Being so close to him tested my willpower.
I wanted to throw myself at him, to wrap my arms
around his trim waist and lay my head on his broad
chest. But I didn't want to make a fool of myself.
What if this was only a social call? Or a visit to
talk about Ethan and Niamh's house? There could
be any number of reasons he was here apart from
the one I hoped.

'Erm…are you here about your handkerchief?'
I asked.

He gave me a blank look. 'What handkerchief?'

'The one you lent me the evening we met Ethan
and Niamh at the restaurant when they announced
their engagement. I should've given it back to you
before now.' I could feel my cheeks heating and
wondered if he knew why I had kept it.

'I'm not here about that.'

'Oh.'

'I've missed you.' His voice was deep and serious, not hint of playfulness now.

I licked my suddenly dry lips. 'I've missed you
too.' Okay, maybe showing a little vulnerability
wasn't too over the top. But I was wary because
what if he just wanted to be friends with benefits? I wanted much more than that. Much more. I
wanted the fairy tale.

He reached out to take my hands in his and I
had to suppress a gasp of pleasure as his fingers
wrapped around mine. His gaze met mine and my

stomach hollowed out at the desperate longing I could see in the grey-blue depths of his eyes.

'I don't think anyone has ever touched me the way you touched me,' he said.

'Yes, well, we did push a few boundaries in the bedroom.' Here's the thing—when I'm nervous I use humour to cover how I'm feeling.

Grayson laughed and tugged me a little closer. 'That's exactly why I love you so much. You constantly make me laugh.'

I stared at him, my mouth hanging open. 'What did you just say?'

'I said, you constantly make me laugh.' His eyes were practically dancing their way out of their sockets and his smile was wider than I had ever seen it before.

'The bit before that…' I moistened my dry lips again, my heart pounding like a drum inside my ribcage.

He squeezed my hands and brought them up to his chest, holding them against the solid steady thud of his heart. 'I love you, my darling.'

I blinked. I blinked again. Could this be really happening? Was I imagining this, or did he just say the words I longed to hear?

'That's what I thought I heard you say, but I wasn't sure if I was dreaming or not.'

'You're not dreaming. This is real. What I feel for you is real. I just wish I had realised earlier. I love you so very much. These past few weeks have been a living torture without you.' He brought his mouth down to mine and kissed me passionately, thoroughly, hungrily.

After a few breathless minutes he pulled back to look down at me again.

'When you said at the wedding that you thought I saw you, the real you, I wasn't ready to admit that you saw the real me too. We have so much in common and yet I was denying the connection from the start, even before we began our fling. I was determined to keep away from you because I think, on a subconscious level, I knew you spelled danger.' He wrapped his arms around me and held me close to his chest, his chin resting on the top of my head. 'I can't believe I let you go like that. I was so stubborn, so scared, to be honest. You threatened me because you opened your heart to me, and I didn't have the courage to open mine to you.'

I lifted my head off his chest to gaze up at him through shimmering eyes. 'I can't believe you love me. I think I fell in love with you when you first kissed me. I tried so hard not to fall for you. I knew it was not part of the deal, that we said no feelings were to be involved, but you made it impossible for me to resist you.'

He smiled and brought one of his hands up to cup my cheek, his eyes meshing with mine. 'I spent a lot of time over the past few weeks thinking about my life. The mistakes I've made in not facing up to what I really want. I'd told myself I didn't want to settle down. I'd seen my parents go through a bitter divorce; I'd seen good friends drift away after Ethan's accident. Love didn't seem something I could rely on. I didn't want to rely on it and get hurt the way my mother and Ethan got hurt. The way I got hurt. But I realise now I need to take the chance because life is not always predicable. Love is what gets you through the unpredictability if you're lucky. And spending that time with you made me see how lucky I was to have you in my life. And I want to keep you in my life. For ever.' His hand moved from my cheek to take something out of his pocket.

I swallowed and stared at the velvet ring box with my heart leaping in my chest. 'Is that what I think it is?'

He grinned and flipped open the lid of the tiny box. 'This ring belonged to my grandmother. She wore it for sixty-two years and loved my grandfather for every single one of them. Will you marry me, my darling girl?'

I couldn't believe what I was hearing. The ring was beautiful—exactly the sort of ring I would have chosen for myself. 'Oh, darling, of course I'll marry you.'

He took the ring out of the box and slipped it on my left hand. I wasn't one bit surprised it was a perfect fit. It seemed to confirm our destiny to be together, the unification of two families who were once bitterly estranged.

'I have to tell you I'm not a fan of long engagements,' Grayson said. 'It only took a couple of weeks to pull off Ethan and Niamh's wedding.'

I laughed and flung my arms around him. 'I can't wait to be your wife. But I don't need a flower-filled church and a choir to be happy. I just need to be with you.'

'How about Vegas?' There was a teasing glint in his eye.

'Funny man. No, I think a beach somewhere with the sun setting in the background as we exchange our vows.'

'Sounds perfect.' He brought his mouth back down to mine in a kiss that was full of love and hope for the future.

After another passionate interlude, Grayson lifted his mouth off mine to gaze into my love-drunk eyes. 'There's another thing we need to discuss. Are we going to have children?'

'Would you like to have them?'

'I always told myself no, but I've been thinking about it a lot lately. Seeing my brother prepare for fatherhood has made me realise what a privilege it is to be a parent. I can't think of anyone I would rather raise a family with than you.'

My heart was so full of love I thought it was going to burst out of my chest.

'I would love that. I was the same, always telling myself I didn't want a family, but that was because I didn't feel like I deserved to have one after what happened to Niamh. But I'm learning to forgive myself. I was just a child and accidents happen even when a parent or other adults are around.'

Grayson held me close again and I felt so secure and safe, ready to face whatever life dished up. We would face it together, not alone. We would be a team working together.

'I'm proud of you for letting go of the past,' he said. 'I've had to do it too. I guess we will always have some measure of guilt about what happened to our siblings, but we can't let it colour our whole life. We owe it to them to live our best lives.' He eased back to look me in the eyes again. 'And my best life is with you.'

\* \* \* \* \*

## #4121 THE MAID MARRIED TO THE BILLIONAIRE
*Cinderella Sisters for Billionaires*
by Lynne Graham
Enigmatic billionaire Enzo discovers Skye frightened and on the run with her tiny siblings. Honorably, Enzo offers them sanctuary and Skye a job. But could their simmering attraction solve another problem—his need for a bride?

## #4122 HIS HOUSEKEEPER'S TWIN BABY CONFESSION
by Abby Green
Housekeeper Carrie wasn't looking for love. Especially with her emotionally guarded boss, Massimo. But when their chemistry ignites on a trip to Buenos Aires, Carrie is left with some shocking news. She's expecting Massimo's twins!

## #4123 IMPOSSIBLE HEIR FOR THE KING
*Innocent Royal Runaways*
by Natalie Anderson
Unwilling to inflict the crown on anyone else, King Niko didn't want a wife. But then he learns of a medical mix-up. Maia, a woman he's never met, is carrying his child! And there's only one way to legitimize his heir...

## #4124 A RING TO CLAIM HER CROWN
by Amanda Cinelli
To become queen, Princess Minerva must marry. So when she sees her ex-fiancé, Liro, among her suitors, she's shocked! The past is raw between them, but the more time she spends in Liro's alluring presence, the more wearing anyone else's ring feels unthinkable...

HPCNMRA0623

### #4125 THE BILLIONAIRE'S ACCIDENTAL LEGACY
*From Destitute to Diamonds*
by Millie Adams

When playboy billionaire Ewan "loses" his Scottish estate to poker pro Jessie, he doesn't expect the sizzling night they end up sharing... So months later when he sees a photo of a very beautiful, very *pregnant* Jessie, a new endgame is required. He's playing for keeps!

### #4126 AWAKENED ON HER ROYAL WEDDING NIGHT
by Dani Collins

Prince Felipe must wed promptly or lose his crown. And though model Claudine is surprised by his proposal, she agrees. She's never felt the kind of searing heat that flashes between them before. But can she enjoy the benefits of their marital bed without catching feelings for her new husband?

### #4127 UNVEILED AS THE ITALIAN'S BRIDE
by Cathy Williams

Dante needs a wife—urgently! And the business magnate looks to the one woman he trusts...his daughter's nanny! It's just a mutually beneficial business arrangement. Until their first kiss after "I do" lifts the veil on an inconvenient, inescapable attraction!

### #4128 THE BOSS'S FORBIDDEN ASSISTANT
by Clare Connelly

Brazilian billionaire Salvador retreated to his private island after experiencing a tragic loss, vowing not to love again. When he's forced to hire a temporary assistant, he's convinced Harper Lawson won't meet his scrupulous standards... Instead, she exceeds them. If only he wasn't drawn to their untamable forbidden chemistry...

---

**YOU CAN FIND MORE INFORMATION ON UPCOMING HARLEQUIN TITLES, FREE EXCERPTS AND MORE AT HARLEQUIN.COM.**

HPCNMRB0623

# Get 3 FREE REWARDS!

**We'll send you 2 FREE Books plus a FREE Mystery Gift.**

**FREE** Value Over **$20**

Both the **Harlequin® Desire** and **Harlequin Presents®** series feature compelling novels filled with passion, sensuality and intriguing scandals.

# HARLEQUIN
## PLUS

Try the best multimedia
subscription service for romance
readers like you!

## Read, Watch and Play.

Experience the easiest way to get
the romance content you crave.

Start your **FREE TRIAL** at
[www.harlequinplus.com/freetrial](www.harlequinplus.com/freetrial).